the miracle girl

A novel by T. B. MARKINSON

Published by T. B. Markinson
Visit T. B. Markinson's official website at tbmarkinson.wordpress.com for the latest news, book details, and other information.

Cover Design by: Erin Dameron-Hill / EDHGraphics
Edited by: Jeri Walker
Proofread by: Kelly Hashway

Prologue

I straddled the naked woman on my bed. Claire's indigo eyes gazed into mine, her expression a mixture of satisfaction tinged with longing.

She let out a contented sigh. "Why didn't we do that years ago?"

I brushed some loose strands of hair off her cheek. "I wanted to from the beginning, but I never knew how to tell you."

Her knowing smile riled me.

"When did you first want to?" I motioned to the tangled sheets.

"To sleep with you?" She raised an eyebrow.

I tickled her sides. "Come on. Spill."

She squirmed underneath me. "Okay. Okay." She put a palm up to indicate surrender. "For some time now. After Andrew and I broke things off last year, I knew I wanted more with you. I just …" She looked away briefly before pinning me with her eyes. "I didn't want to complicate our friendship in case …" She shrugged while fidgeting with the knotted friendship bracelet on my left wrist.

I nodded. That was the big reason why I never confessed my love. And my fear of her not feeling the same. In the past, girls had felt overwhelmed by my intensity. When I loved someone, I loved them with a passion. Fearful that I would drive Claire away, I tamped that intensity down to the best of my abilities, denying how much I wanted to be with her.

In a moment of weakness earlier that evening, I had kissed her on the cheek. Surprisingly, Claire kissed me back on the lips. Before I knew what was happening, we were ripping each other's clothes off.

"Crappy timing, really," she said.

"What do you mean?" I asked, knowing full well what she meant.

"You're leaving tomorrow, remember?" Her voice hardened as she spoke.

"I won't be gone that long."

Her narrowed eyes told me otherwise.

"Why don't you come with me?"

Claire pushed me off her. "What? Go to Europe for six months?"

"Yes! We'll have a blast." I wasn't peeved in the slightest that she had shoved me off. Claire could always be kinda prickly. When she turned around I finally saw all the color seeping out of her face like shower water slipping through the drain.

"You're crazy if you think I'm going with you." Claire stood and yanked on a T-shirt. In her hurry she put on mine instead of her own, but I didn't think it was the right time to bring that to her attention.

Her colorless face spooked me. But the drastic change in Claire's demeanor caused bells to jingle in my head. It felt like twenty church towers resided inside me, and each and every one had a demented Quasimodo pulling desperately on the cords for the bells announcing the end of the world. "What's wrong? Why are you getting dressed?"

"This was a mistake. I'm sorry. I should have known." She fumbled around looking for her jeans.

"What was a mistake? This?" Once again, I pointed to the bed.

Earlier that night, both of us had walked across the stage to receive our degrees. I received one in journalism, and Claire a business degree. She had some job interviews set up for the following week, while I was heading to Europe to backpack for six months. It was my graduation gift from my parents. They had started putting money into a college account before I was born, and when I received a full four-year ride, they decided to give me the money when I graduated. My desire was to see a bit of the world before I started a career.

Claire let out a long breath. "I'm sorry, JJ. I love you. I really do. But I need more stability in my life. Not a gypsy."

"Gypsy!" I couldn't help laughing at the idea and fell back onto the bed. I wasn't loaded, but I'd never struggled financially. When I returned from Europe my father had a job lined up for me at the Denver newspaper where he worked. He was a sportswriter and arranged for me to start in the advertising department. Not my ideal job, but it was a job nonetheless during times when not many graduates had one lined up. At least it wasn't the mailroom.

"I shouldn't have started something I knew wouldn't go anywhere. This was too risky." Claire sat heavily on the couch on the far side of the room, shaking. My studio apartment didn't allow much room for escape.

"This? You mean I'm a risk?" I placed a hand on my chest. "Or do you mean being with a woman?" I slipped her T-shirt over my head and wrapped my arms tightly around my chest, suddenly feeling exposed and vulnerable in the small space.

"You know I don't give a crap about being with women or with men. You're not the first woman I've slept with. You know that."

"Yes, but you've never had a serious relationship with a woman. You've only been serious with Andrew."

Andrew had been Claire's boyfriend during most of her undergrad. He was a bit of a prick, but I tolerated him for Claire's sake. I never let on that I was in love with Claire, and Andrew never suspected.

"Andrew asked me to marry him. I wasn't sure at first, but ..."

A huff of air tore from my body as if someone had struck me across the chest with a baseball bat.

When Andrew graduated last year, he had decided to sow his wild oats. Apparently, he was now changing his tune, but this was the first time I had heard of it.

"Was that what this was? You slept with me to get back at Andrew for fucking around before he decided it was time to settle down? Are you trying to even the score? Or did you need to find out something first?"

Claire threw a random shoe at my head and missed by a mile. "Fuck you. At least with him I know where I stand. You aren't really the commitment type. When's the last time you were in a relationship that lasted longer than three months?"

"That's because I was in love with you. No one has compared." I walked up to Claire and wrapped her in my arms, convinced I could talk some sense into her like usual. She always spooked easily, and normally I could talk her off the ledge. At first, Claire melted into my embrace, but the moment didn't last. I felt the muscles in her shoulders tense, indicating she had made up her mind to toss me aside without ever giving me a chance. I wanted to laugh in her face if she thought Andrew would treat her better. No one would ever love her as much as I did.

Claire leaned away, putting her palms up to indicate she wanted space. "You can't even commit to your name."

"What?" I didn't attempt to hide my confusion.

"JJ? To this day I don't know what the initials stand for." Claire pinned me with a knowing look like she had cracked some secret code.

"Jamilla Jean. You never asked. Everyone calls me JJ." When I was called to accept my degree earlier that night, the announcer had said JJ Cavendish. That was how everyone knew me.

"That's a lovely name. You should grow up, Jamilla Jean." Claire slipped on a black boot.

"Me? You want Andrew to take care of you. That's why you're doing this. You think I'm too much of a risk. Why? Because you actually love me. You can't tell me that you love Andrew. If you did, you wouldn't have seduced me earlier."

"I seduced you?" She ran her hand angrily through her hair. "This is why I didn't want to go down this path."

"*This path*," I parroted. "You can lie to yourself, Claire, but you can't lie to me. I see it in your eyes. I know you're in love with me. I also see the fear."

Claire bit her trembling lower lip.

"No one will love you as much as I do, and that scares the crap out of you." I reached for her arm, but she pulled away.

"Love isn't the answer to everything. What about stability? Permanence? For as long as I've known you, you're always in motion. Never settling down. What kind of life can you offer? Do you think we can survive on love? Do you want me to always wait while you go off on one of those adventures you're always talking about? You're the one who wants to gallivant around the globe, searching for stories. Me, I want normal. A home, family … roots." She shook her head remorsefully. "I just don't think it'll work. And with you running off to Europe and leaving me behind …" Her words trailed off, but not her sentiment.

"So that's that. You'd rather settle with Andrew."

"Settle? Andrew has a great job with a lot of prospects. What can you offer? We both know you won't stick around long at the advertising job your dad got you. You and advertising? You and a job—can you convince me you won't dash off the first chance you get? Jesus, for the past four years, you've hopped in your car come every chance to find some type of adventure." Claire's piercing eyes waited for my response.

I didn't have one.

"That's what I thought. You're always full of promises and grandiose ideas, but actions. Actions. Stop saying you're going to be someone. Do it!"

I stumbled back, as if Claire had hit me with an uppercut, gasping for breath. Eventually, I found the strength to roar, "Get out!"

The triumph in Claire's eyes faded into shame. I could see this wasn't how she wanted things to end. But my wounded pride wouldn't take the words back. Part of me screamed to rush to her, force her to stay and talk things over. The other part said run. Run far away.

When I heard the click of the front door, I felt as if my leg muscles disintegrated. I sat on the floor in a pile of our remaining clothes and flashed back to the moment when she had kissed me. God, it had felt like everything was right with the world. I finally had Claire.

My Claire.

Four hours later, she was gone. Gone for good, it seemed. I clutched her sweater and smelled her perfume and the all-too-familiar scent of Tide. Her clothes always smelled like Tide. All these years, her mom did her laundry. It wasn't a secret that Claire wasn't a self-sufficient woman. She'd gotten through college well enough, but her parents lived only an hour away. Every weekend Claire dropped off her laundry, which her mother washed, ironed, and folded. And her mother prepared home-cooked meals that Claire pulled out of the freezer each night. Her father managed her checking account. Claire had never been accountable for anything in her life.

Let her marry Andrew. He had a promising engineering career ahead of him. He was stable, and Claire liked the way that made her feel. She had said it again and again over the years. She was never hot and heavy for

Andrew, but comfortable around him. That was what she wanted. Comfort. Stability. Easy. Three things I never wanted. I craved passion, thrills, and momentum.

Maybe it was best to make a clean break. College was over. Like she said, time to grow up.

I wiped my eyes, determined to be strong. A small object by the door caught my attention. It took me a second or two to finally figure out what it was. Claire's matching friendship bracelet, the one we made our first summer together when we were co-counselors for a day camp. Since the day we had made them, neither one of us had taken them off. That was her parting gift: a clean break.

I snatched her bracelet from the floor and then yanked mine off. While rolling both of them in my fingers, I made a decision.

Yes, it was time for me to grow up. Leave my college love behind. Move on with my life.

The next morning I boarded a plane and never intended to see Claire again. It wasn't until the plane took off that I realized I had made a terrible mistake, but it was too late. Or so I thought.

Running was easier.

chapter one

I stood in my new office. The view, while nice, wasn't spectacular. In New York City, I had an incredible view of Central Park from my Fifth Avenue office located on the twenty-seventh floor. Here, in Denver, I could see the foothills of the Rocky Mountains from the third floor. It wasn't the view that bothered me. It was the new job.

Mile High News was a dying newspaper. The higher-ups at Beale Media Corp almost believed it was a foregone conclusion that the doors would close by the end of the year. It was the first of February and, by the looks of the trees, everything seemed bleak. But, Cora Matthews, the woman in charge, had sent me here, her "miracle" girl, just in case this office could be turned around. My deadline was December thirty-first. Cora, who was not only my boss, but my mentor and friend from my first days with the company, wasn't even giving me a full year.

I sighed, resting my head on the cool glass of the window, hoping it would soothe the tension.

This medium-sized paper employed three hundred people full-time and had dozens of part-time workers and freelance journalists, not to mention all the carriers and delivery drivers who pulled themselves out of their warm beds at ungodly hours in all types of weather to deliver papers. Over a hundred thousand subscribers relied on us for their news. In New York at *The Beale Chronicle*, one of the oldest papers in the country still in existence, I had a staff three times the size, and the print circulation was closer to a million with several million online subscribers worldwide. But Denver was different. I was born and raised here. These people were my people, and I felt a greater responsibility to save *Mile High*.

I had left Colorado twenty-something years ago after graduating from college. Since then I completed my masters in journalism at Columbia, and five years later, under Cora's direction, I received an MBA from Harvard. Hard to believe I'd started as a freelance travel writer. Cora was the one who gave me my first break. She saw my passion for travel and loved my ability to weave stories in a way that always pulled in readers. Cora also saw I understood the business. After three years, I was working full-time for the New York paper. I still went on travel assignments, but she'd started to trust me with the business side. Now Beale Media Corp was grooming me, Cora's Miracle Girl, to take over some day. Failing in Denver wouldn't look good.

That wasn't the only aspect that drove me to succeed. When I left, I was a no one. A scared kid who wanted to be someone. Now I was someone and wanted to prove that in my hometown.

My father no longer worked at *Mile High*, but that didn't mean I didn't feel a strong connection to the paper and to the people who worked their asses off every single day to put out an entirely brand new product seven days a week. Most people didn't think about that. All the offices all over the country had deadlines throughout the day that had to be met, no matter what. Each time a paper was sent to the presses was a miracle in its own right. Coordinating the news, advertisements, obituaries, classifieds, flyers, local announcements … the list went on and on … was not an easy process. And staffs managed it every single day, 365 days a year.

Today was my first "real" day on the job, even though I'd been cramming in as much information as humanly possible ever since I heard last week I was being transferred home.

Home.

Another sigh escaped my lips.

I had left Colorado the day after I finished my undergraduate degree and never looked back. It was too painful to remember that last night with Claire. The first and last time we made love. The night she told me I was too much of a risk.

Now, standing in my office in Denver I felt like an outsider. Over the years I had lived in New York City, Boston, London, and Chicago. Plus several short stints in cities all over the world. Occasionally, I came home to visit my parents, but as was more often the case, I flew them out to meet me in whatever city I was in at the moment. It was less painful that way. Colorado reminded me of Claire.

As soon as the plane had touched down at Denver International Airport, the idea of Claire infiltrated my heart and soul. Everywhere I looked, I saw Claire. Every scent reminded me of a past memory. Every sound. Jesus Christ, I was becoming a walking cliché for lovesick fools. I stifled a groan.

I laughed out loud when I remembered her telling me to grow up and accept my name, Jamilla Jean. My parents had stuck me with a stupid name to avoid a family dispute, but no one had ever called me by my real name. No one. Jamilla Jean was a mouthful. My parents felt compelled to name me after both of their mothers. Even though they put the names on the birth certificate, I was branded JJ since the day I popped out. My grandmothers understood since neither of them liked their names either. They never broke the unspoken agreement. Having their names on the certificate was victory enough, but why they desired to have me named after them was a mystery. Aiming for a bit of immortality, I guessed.

I looked at the foothills and wondered what Claire was doing right then. Did she ever think of me? Did she ever wonder *what if?*

Over the years I had dated off and on. At one point I thought I'd found the one, but the relationship fizzled after three years. Nothing spectacular happened. We just both woke up and realized we were trying to force something that wasn't there in the first place. I was finally at peace with the reality that I would be alone with the exception of the occasional fling. Not everyone found their soul mate, or more aptly, not everyone was able to hold on to them.

Someone coughed behind me. I turned around to see my new assistant, Avery Fleischer, standing in the doorway. At first glance, Avery was an intimidating woman. A black belt in karate, she had recently returned from three weeks in Israel, where she attended an intensive and elite Krav Maga training program. Her black hair was slicked back into a ponytail. With her intense stare and rigid posture, she looked like she should be protecting the

President of the United States. She was like a chameleon and could fill many roles: protector, business woman, spy, and so much more.

"I'm sorry to bother you, Ms. Cavendish, but they're ready downstairs." Avery flashed an apologetic, uncertain smile that managed to come across as confident. Her sweet voice didn't fit her physical prowess. I wondered if this was part of her training. She was slightly taller than I was, meaning she was still considered short by most, considering my petite frame.

"Yes, of course, Avery. Thank you, and please call me JJ." I turned from the ambitious twenty-seven-year-old. Avery had moved with me from New York and had never been west of the Mississippi. She was a New Yorker, through and through. Why the higher-ups had sent an "outsider" to Denver, Colorado baffled me. Not that Denver was a cultural backwater. Colorado was an interesting mix of new and old. Denver was progressive, but a drive to some of the outlying rural areas less than thirty miles away still felt like stepping back a few decades. Avery had never been to Buffalo, New York, let alone a city like Denver. She knew two places well: Israel and New York City. We hadn't worked closely back East, but I admired the young woman from afar.

Young woman. I chuckled to myself in the elevator, turning my head so Avery wouldn't see. Young woman ... I was only forty-four. Not that much older. At least I didn't feel that much older—most days.

No one, except the people in the know, had any idea that I was in the building already. The vice president of the company wanted to make the announcement to the entire staff of *Mile High* at a morning meeting. The previous publisher, a fifty-year-old New Jersey man named Henry Wilcox, wasn't popular and had only lasted seven months. The staff rebelled against the outsider who didn't understand their ways and the ways of the West. According to Cora, he was too blunt, caustic, and demanding. The New Jersey man had kept trying to ram down everyone's throat how things were done in the East. He came across more like Tony Soprano and not a refined publisher. The staff thought their ways were just fine. Henry countered by saying if that was the case why did they have to lay off fifty people the previous quarter. He continued by stating the obvious: the paper was dying and there was no way around it. Even if the assessment was correct, his lack of tact was detrimental to his success. Cora wanted me to use more finesse.

You could say those things where he came from since folks were used to leaders with an iron fist. You couldn't in Denver. Here, people were polite. If you stumbled upon someone on the sidewalk, it was customary to say hello and possibly stop to chat about the weather. Coloradoans love to discuss the weather. Some days all four seasons could be experienced in a span of twelve hours and, even though this happened all of the time, it still fascinated them. New Yorkers never stopped for idle chitchat. Hell, even making eye contact was unusual. If one did and then added a hello, the recipient would cringe and more than likely consider the friendly person a fruitcake or a deranged psychopath.

The higher-ups realized they needed an insider to save the paper if that was possible. I questioned their motives. I hadn't been home, except for the occasional quick trip to say hello to my folks, in twenty years. What did I know about Colorado anymore? I could discuss the mating habits of lions, or describe walking through the spray of Victoria Falls, but the Denver Broncos, Greeley Stampede days, ski reports, and a million other things associated with my home state now escaped me. Cora disagreed and told me to pack my bags. I had one week before I started my new job.

It wasn't the first time I'd been shipped off to a fledging office. But it was the first time I was to become the publisher and stay for a while. Usually I arrived, assessed the situation, helped trim the fat, and put an action plan in motion to get them back on track or to close the doors.

I stood off to the side out of sight as I listened to the vice president's introduction. Hearing people describe me to a large group was an uncomfortable experience. "She has an incredible knack for being at the right place at the right time. Over twenty years ago, she was in Berlin when the wall fell down."

I thought about my backpacking trip in Europe. What that had cost me. Bill Trent, the vice president of Beale Media Corp, was touting Berlin as one of the greatest triumphs in my life. No one knew the truth, not even my parents, whom I was extremely close with, but I could never tell them how close I came to staying in Colorado. My parents were proud of my achievements, but I knew deep down they wished I had stayed home. They loved visiting with me all over the world, but ultimately how many parents wanted their child thousands of miles away?

Bill rambled on about other achievements in my career. I knew he was close to his favorite part. I braced for it. "The CEO of the company, Cora Matthews, has sent JJ the Miracle Girl to turn things around here. Ladies and gentlemen, please welcome JJ Cavendish." The vice president turned to me, clapping. I stood frozen. Miracle girl. Why did everyone have to seize on the nickname Cora had given me years ago? Just thinking about the reason …

Avery nudged me forward with her shoulder, and I went into business mode. Many didn't realize that being a good boss meant one had to be a good showman. I tugged my black blazer to ensure it was straight and stepped onto the stage to speak to the staff.

"Thanks, Bill, for all the kind words, and at least sixty-five percent was true." Bill laughed heartily, and the crowd joined in.

I turned to the employees sitting on folding chairs in the small auditorium, and as I spoke my eyes wandered over their faces. Eye contact was another key to success. People wanted to feel a connection. Slowly, I prattled on about how we would make a good team. I had given this speech so many times I didn't have to think. My brain switched to autopilot. I used to travel the world for stories. Now I traveled to cities to save or cut jobs.

Then I saw her.

No, it couldn't be. I always thought I saw Claire. Sometimes when getting out of a cab in New York I would sprint after a woman, convinced it was Claire, only to be disappointed.

Claire was gone. That dream was dead.

I squinted to shield my eyes from the stage lights.

It was Claire.

Some murmuring came from the crowd, and I realized I had stopped speaking. Smiling awkwardly, I said, "Sorry, it's just a bit overwhelming to be back home. It's been such a long time. And to be in a room of people I feel like I know already and want to become reacquainted with … well, it's awesome." I spoke these words directly to Claire. When we were in school, Claire loved the word awesome. Everything was awesome.

Standing there, less than fifty feet from her, I remembered her twenty-first birthday. She was never one for presents unless it was a tiny trinket. On her twenty-first I wrapped twenty-one gifts. Small mementos, such as a shot glass I stole from a bar we went to our freshman year. I could still hear her voice, "Oh, JJ, this is the most awesome birthday ever!"

Bill stepped up, sensing he needed to come to my rescue. I was floundering and not making any sense. *Did I just say, "It's awesome?"* This wasn't the type of introduction headquarters wanted me to make.

He patted me on the back. "If I know JJ, she was up all night reading reports." He let out a fake laugh, and some of the brownnosers in the crowd joined in. "Please help yourselves to the donuts and coffee." Bill motioned to the tables in the back, and it didn't take long for the vultures to pounce on the free food, forgetting all about me, their fledging boss who couldn't make it through a speech she could give on her death bed.

Bill turned to me once the coast was clear. "You okay?"

I laughed confidently and waved his concern away. "Yeah. I'm fine. Shall we mingle?" I took a deep cleansing breath and focused on the job at hand.

To his relief, I instantly disappeared into the crowd to meet the workers, doing my best to block out all thoughts of Claire. At least for the next twenty or thirty minutes.

I shook someone's hand and concentrated when he told me his name was George Trindal and he was the head of local news. Before the week was out, I intended to know everyone by name. This was one of my special skills: remembering employees' names, the names of their children, their pets' names, where they went to school, and their hobbies.

It didn't take me long to settle into my groove. I noticed Claire watching from across the room. She nonchalantly made her way toward me and the small gathering. She was slender and barely looked a day over forty, even though I knew she was forty-four. Whatever she was doing to stay young was working. A group of people hung on my every word. Claire rolled her eyes, and I wondered if she was thinking that I hadn't changed one bit. Back in the day, I was always the center of attention. Of course my reasoning had changed. In college I wanted to impress Claire. Today, I told stories about my adventures to avoid talking about my true self. I wanted to remain as anonymous as possible for someone who was often in the limelight, so I selected stories that wowed the crowd without revealing personal details about my life or past. As much as I hated the Miracle Girl label, I used it to my advantage to keep the real meaning hidden and the real me in the shadows.

"So there I was in my room in Zambia … did I mention it didn't have a wall at all in the front?" I paused to make sure the impact of my words sunk in. "It was about ten o'clock at night and even though it was freezing—"

"Freezing? I thought it was hot there." Brenda, the circulation director, interrupted. Her hair resembled a rat's nest, and the bags under her eyes testified that she was a legit circulation director. Out of bed hours before normal people to ensure all the papers were delivered.

"I was there during the winter, and let me tell you, at night it gets bloody cold."

Again Claire rolled her eyes. Was it my use of the word bloody? After spending two years in London for Beale Media Corp more than a decade ago, I couldn't get out of the habit of using certain English words and phrases. I needed to be careful here. Coloradoans wouldn't take to this. Not that they would hate an English person, but an American speaking like a Brit, that wouldn't fly.

"Does it warm up during the day?" pushed Brenda.

I smiled at the woman, sensing she must be this nosy about everything, not just Africa. I would need to be careful around her. So far her questions were neutral, but my gut told me she was used to asking completely inappropriate questions in front of large groups. Maybe that was why she was stuck in circulation. "Yep. On average it was about seventy degrees during the day and then—"

"Bloody cold at night," Brenda interrupted again. Everyone was in a good mood, with the free donuts and coffee, so no one minded Brenda's second interruption. Was this always the case? Brenda motioned for me to continue, which caused a smile to flit across Claire's face. Claire's eyes seemed wiser. No that wasn't right. They seemed like she had grown up. As if she'd become her own woman, not one defined by those around her. I gave a slight tip of the head in Claire's direction, but quickly looked back to the group. She looked stunning in her black pantsuit, and if she'd dressed like that back in the day, I would have tried harder to gain her affection. Success suited Claire. She exuded a calm confidence, and that turned me on.

"Where was I?" Again I paused for effect, regretting doing so instantly. Claire would know what I was up to, and that put me on edge.

"Yes, it was late at night and I was freezing to death. But I got this idea in my head that I wanted to take a bath in the middle of the African Bush, so I turned the water on as hot as it would go and eased in inch by inch.

"The company put me up in this posh resort for a fluff travel piece." I flinched when I said posh, not remembering if that was strictly an English word or if people across the pond used it now. "As I soaked in the tub, which was hidden behind this massive bed draped in elaborate mosquito netting that would have impressed the Queen of England, I sipped a glass of red wine and listened to Victoria Falls off in the distance. I remember thinking that life didn't get much better than that." Another pause, and then I added, "Then I heard it."

Brenda couldn't contain herself and asked, "Heard what?" She took another bite of her second donut, chewing with her mouth open.

"A lion."

Everyone gasped.

"Was it in the room?" asked George, as he nervously peeked around the room like the lion might magically appear.

"And you were naked?" queried Tim, an ads salesman. Even before he asked if I was naked I got the sense that he was a perv from the way he undressed all the women with his eyes, including Brenda. I almost punched him in the face when I saw him ogle Claire. He raised his coffee to his lips, and I focused on his hairy knuckles. Ugh!

The group chuckled, and I blushed faintly. That was one of the dangers of telling this particular story to a large group. Odds were there was at least one perv.

"Yes, Tim, completely naked." I turned to George. "And no, the lion wasn't in the room. But this lion roared, and when I say roared, I mean roared!"

"Were you all alone?" asked Brenda.

"I was." I confirmed before taking a sip of my coffee, already bored with this story. How many times had I told it now? Ten? Twenty? Probably more. I almost laughed out loud thinking of the tiny voice in my head saying, "Focus on the lion, folks. Not on JJ."

I noticed with amusement that the younger eyes in the group showed disappointment that there was no real danger, and the older eyes glowed with envy over the luxury of taking a bath in the Bush. Perception changed drastically with age. The young always had notions of romance and adventure. The older folks seemed to relish independence and adventure.

"Were you scared?" asked George, who looked like he would have been.

"No. It was probably one of the most exhilarating experiences I've ever had. They say you can hear a lion's roar several miles away, so odds were I wasn't in any real danger." I shrugged, and Bill approached the group, towering over everyone in his three-piece suit. A former NBA star, Bill got into the media biz when he blew his knee after only three years with the Knicks.

"Did you tell them yet about the bear that attacked you?" Bill beamed over my ability to win people over, but I gathered he was trying to send me a message: tell stories about Colorado or the West, not Zambia. I bobbed my head slightly, indicating I understood. Bill's swift nod back told me not to worry. One hour on the job and I already had the staff eating out of the palm of my hand. Just what headquarters wanted. An insider, who could also impress them. From the glint in his eyes, he'd already forgotten about my flubbed speech.

"Not yet." I smiled, knowing he was about to whisk me away, luckily.

"Next time. I hate to do this folks, but JJ has a meeting with the mayor." Bill motioned for me to walk before him to the elevator.

There was some grumbling. Not only would they miss out on the bear story, but it also meant they had to return to work.

Before allowing myself to be ushered away, I said, "No worries, I'll tell you all soon. I would like to thank all of you for making me feel so welcome. This has been one of the most pleasant meetings I've had in a long time." I half covered my mouth, giving the impression I didn't want Bill and Avery to hear, and whispered conspiratorially, "It's been years since I felt so comfortable. I'm used to East Coast people." I winked.

With that, I made my exit. When Bill and Avery weren't looking, I glanced back to see Brenda loop her arm through Claire's, and they shared a laugh. Interesting, but not surprising. My gut told me that Brenda was the freak at the paper, and Claire had a soft spot for underdogs, always befriending the friendless.

Bill contained his smile until we were alone in the elevator. "Nice touch, Miracle Girl."

I cringed, not that he noticed. He and Avery were too busy typing on their company-issued Blackberries. At sixty-three, Bill wasn't up with the times and only used his Blackberry. Watching the man hunt and peck on his laptop with his index fingers was painful. Bill's way with people was how he'd climbed the corporate ladder. Kung Fu Avery's brain and work ethic had gotten her here. She had her iPhone stacked underneath her company cell, and underneath both was her iPad. There were times when I saw her typing on one of her phones and on her iPad simultaneously, baffling me that she could manage. She could possibly become the youngest CEO of the company. Cora taught me early on that I should never fear having competent people around. Surround myself with the best and reap the rewards as the team leader.

chapter two

The following morning, after a day filled with tedious meet-and-greet appointments, I pulled into the parking lot at 5:30 a.m. I was wiped out. After returning to my hotel the previous night, I sat on the balcony and replayed that last night with Claire in my head. Not just the leaving, but the whole night, trying to pinpoint exactly where I went wrong. It was torture, and my therapist would have reprimanded me if she knew. Living in the past wouldn't help me conquer my demons and move forward.

Sitting in my car, I reached down deep to find the strength to head to my office and become JJ Cavendish, the publisher. Not many knew I started my day before sunrise. It was a habit I began right from the start. I was careful not to send too many e-mails before 7:00 a.m. except to those I wanted to impress, but I drafted all of my e-mails first thing and then sent them out promptly at seven. In the beginning I did this so I wouldn't come across as trying too hard, except to those who needed to be dazzled. Now I enjoyed keeping my secret. I didn't like to share a lot about myself, really. I spun a few yarns now and then about my travels to maintain an image, but my personal life was out of the question, and that included the fact that I was a morning person.

I thought about the day before and the stories I'd told at the meeting. That was what people had come to expect. They liked to hear about adventure. In my younger days, I craved adventure, always willing to travel for a story or escape. I escaped a lot. Now, I wanted quiet. Not that my job would give me much peace. People then and now never really wanted to get to know me. Not many knew that I liked my coffee with two sugars, had a dog named Sinclair (who'd passed away from cancer one month prior to my move), and that I preferred to be in bed each night before ten unless there was a work emergency or function. When emergencies happened, I slept in my office where I always kept at least one change of clothes.

In my opinion, my everyday life was like anyone else's—everyday. At least to those who worked in the media biz. But over the years the company had built up my reputation to be this dynamic employee and worldwide adventurer. Exciting, competent, and successful. I felt like I had to be "on" every second at work. A larger-than-life female Hemingway. Bolstering this image that Cora framed for me helped my career, but not my soul.

The couple of hours I was allowed to work in private in the morning were my most productive and satisfying.

I slipped in through the back door, unnoticed. The building never shut down completely, not even on Christmas. Most employees didn't notice others who came and went early in the morning since there were always people going in and out of the building. The joy of the newspaper business never stopped.

Some lights were on in the office. Mostly in the advertising section, which took up two-thirds of the first floor. Circulation and the front desk were hidden from my viewpoint by the backstairs leading to my office on the third floor. More than likely only graphic designers were present, building ads that would appear in tomorrow's paper.

I paused and studied the advertising department. So many years ago, I was supposed to start my first job here after college. How would that have changed my life? Sighing, I turned to ascend the backstairs to my office, but a flicker of light in the only office in the advertising department caught my attention. All the other desks were out in the open. It had to be Claire. Yesterday I had found out she was the director of advertising.

Back in college Claire was not a morning person. She was famous for being the exact opposite: staying up till two or three and never having any classes before noon. Remembering this, I couldn't help but wonder why she was in the office so early.

Curiosity got the best of me. I released the handrail, turned around, and marched to her office. And truth be known, I didn't want to pass up the opportunity to finally speak to her alone after all these years.

Her windowless office, with a massive desk and file cabinets along the side screamed that the occupant didn't care about showmanship. This wasn't a gathering place to woo prospective clients. This was a place for Claire to get down to the nitty-gritty of running the advertising department. I was immediately impressed.

"Are you always here this early?" I asked.

Claire nearly jumped out of her skin. "Fuck!" She swiveled around quickly in her chair and saw me, her new boss, and her mottled cheeks showed embarrassment. "I'm sorry. Y-you startled me."

I couldn't contain a smile. "I should apologize. You always were jumpy. Do you remember when you pulled a muscle during the movie *Misery*?" I grinned at the memory, and I knew I looked like that lovesick puppy that used to follow her everywhere. I didn't give a damn.

"That Annie was one scary bitch." Again it looked like Claire felt like an idiot for saying bitch in front of the publisher of the paper.

"That's putting it mildly." I set my leather briefcase down and leaned against the doorjamb. "So are you?"

"Am I what?" Claire scrunched up her face, reminding me just why I had loved this woman so many years ago. Even with her face all distorted, Claire was lovely. Her auburn hair, full lips, and sapphire eyes. Not to mention her wondrous tits. Claire's blouse was undone at the top, and from my angle I had a fantastic view. Voluptuous didn't begin to describe them.

"Are you always here this early?" I pulled my eyes off her chest. Feeling warm, I shrugged off my blazer.

"Normally. I like the quiet time. I live around the corner from my parents, so my mom, who loves mornings more than you do, comes over to get my son ready for school."

Son. Claire had a son.

I smiled broadly, trying to cover my disappointment. I had hoped Claire wouldn't be married, even if that was a selfish thought.

"What's his name?"

"Ian."

"How old is he?"

"Six."

I didn't want to know but felt compelled to ask, "How is Andrew?"

Claire stared dumbfounded before she recovered and mumbled, "He's fine."

Her brief answer intrigued me. The previous night I had intended to google Claire and Andrew, but both my personal phone and Blackberry were dead, and I apparently lost my chargers in the move. Plus, the IT department was working on my laptop so I could have access to everything at *Mile High*. It was an eerie night since I was hardly ever unplugged.

Claire motioned to a bag of M&Ms on her desk. "Want some?"

This made me smile. "I see you're still addicted. Do you still eat two at a time and never the same color at once?"

To answer my question, she popped a blue and green M&M into her mouth.

We remained quiet for several uncomfortable seconds.

"What about you?" asked Claire. She leaned back in her desk chair, spoiling my view down her shirt.

I assumed she meant, was I always here so early, since she knew I wasn't a fan of chocolate. "Yes, I'm always in this early, but don't tell anyone or they'll want me to work more." I winked at Claire.

Claire smiled. "Your secret is safe with me. But I meant do you have any … uh, children or a partner?"

I shook my head. "No children, and at the moment, I'm single." I didn't understand why Claire's eyes looked relieved. Did she think I would be an unfit mother? Or a bad partner?

Then the look of relief was replaced with a sympathetic air. "I'm sorry."

"Don't be. I have a dog." Immediately I felt like an ass. "Had a dog. He died recently," I added, averting my eyes briefly.

She grimaced at first like she didn't know what to say. "A dog. You?"

"What do you mean by that?" I feigned being hurt.

"Well, I never pegged you as a dog person … back then." Claire stumbled over the words.

"My parents thought it would be good for me, so they encouraged me to adopt one. Have some stability at home."

"What was your dog's name?" Claire's eyes sparkled.

"Sinclair."

"Upton Sinclair?"

I nodded sheepishly. I always admired the muckraker. And the name reminded me of Claire without being too obvious about it.

"How are your parents?" I had always liked Claire's family and was desperate to prolong our conversation. I wasn't surprised they lived so close to Claire, especially now that they had a grandson.

"Mom is tickled pink over Ian. My brother still hasn't settled down. Dad keeps threatening to retire, and Mom worries it will end their relationship. The man doesn't have any hobbies." Claire smiled. "She bought him and Ian fishing poles. So far the ploy hasn't worked. Ian can't hold still for five minutes, and Dad hates fish and being outdoors."

She was the same old Claire. In under two minutes I felt like I was completely caught up with her life. "I'm with him on that," I said, referring to her father.

"What? Can't hold still or the fish bit?" Claire teased, knowing my answer.

"Fish."

"How's your family?"

"Good. Mom and Pops still live in the same house. All of my aunts and uncles have skedaddled, and I hardly ever see them or my cousins anymore. Family reunions are hard to plan when almost every member besides my parents is roaming here and there."

"Wandering has always been in your blood." Her soft eyes didn't judge.

I started to gather my blazer and briefcase. "I probably should beat it before others see me." I started to leave and then turned abruptly. "We should do lunch." Before Claire had a chance to reply, I was halfway to the back staircase, which was located conveniently close to her office.

I didn't flip on my office light, preferring the illuminated computer screen as the only source. For years I had struggled with migraines and tried to avoid brightness, even dimming my computer screen as much as possible.

My e-mail inbox was flooded per usual. Normally I jumped right in. I enjoyed zapping the useless e-mails that contained reports the higher-ups thrived on, but either didn't include the pertinent information or presented it all wrong. Not all reports were a waste of time. I knew one of my first tasks would be to whittle down what was needed, what was superfluous, and how to package it better. If I was going to save this paper, I had to cut the fat. Not everyone would be onboard with that, of course.

Darrell Miller, the managing editor, was the biggest obstacle, and headquarters already had given their blessing to do away with him—not immediately, to keep the gossip mill quiet for the initial transition, yet as soon as possible. He used to be a rock star in the newspaper world until something happened to him about ten years ago, right about the time his wife left him. Darrell became bitter, impossible to work with, and his writers could never please him. Cora had summoned him more than once to the New York offices to reason with him. To remind him of what he used to be, but to no avail. He seemed dead set on driving the news department into the ground instead of getting on board with the drastic changes of how people consume news and what type of news they hunger after. He probably watched *All the President's Men* every weekend to relive the good old days of Woodward and Bernstein.

He wasn't my only concern. Many of the employees held onto silly tasks out of fear that if their usual responsibilities weren't useful, they'd be let go. I had to find a way to ease their apprehension and get them to see the light. My goal was to save every single job, except for Darrell's. I wouldn't announce that though. A promise like that invited trouble, especially since the decision to lay off people rested with the corporate office ninety percent of the time.

I turned my chair and stared at the foothills. I hadn't expected to see Claire first thing this morning. I hadn't expected to see Claire at all when I first learned of my assignment. How could I have known she worked at the paper? We hadn't spoken since that night.

What happened?

I also expected her child to be older than six. Why had she waited so long? Money? Health issues?

An idea struck, and I pounced on my mouse to bring up the Who's Who page on the company website.

When the name popped up, I stared at the screen like I'd seen a monkey jump out.

Claire Nicholls.

Nicholls? She'd kept her maiden name. That seemed unlike her. She wasn't a feminist by any stretch of the imagination.

I googled Claire Nicholls and found her Facebook page rather easily. There weren't too many people named Claire in Denver, Colorado.

The few photos only showed her son, who was the spitting image of Claire. There was no mention of a spouse, and her status didn't say if she was single, married, divorced … nothing.

Before I could research Andrew, the shrill ring of my desk phone pulled me out of la-la land.

"Hello."

"Ah, JJ, I wasn't expecting you to be in yet," said Bill. "You getting settled into your new office?"

I knew that wasn't the purpose of the call, so I kept my reply brief. "Yes. How was your flight?" Bill's flight had left at midnight, getting him into New York around six so he could rush home, and in his own words "shit, shower, and shave, and be in the office by nine." For a man nearing retirement, he still acted like he was twenty.

"Great. Just great. We landed not long ago at JFK, and I'm on my way to the office. I planned to leave a voicemail, but now that I have you, I wanted to run a few things by you. Do you have a moment?"

A moment. This brought a smile to my face. Bill was good at his job, but keeping things brief wasn't his strong suit. I regretted wasting my morning searching for Claire on the Internet and daydreaming since I knew I'd be on the phone with Bill for at least an hour, probably two. My first full day in the office and I felt like I was three days behind.

"Of course, Bill. Shoot." I gripped my fountain pen ready to use shorthand to jot down every word Bill uttered. Afterwards, I would have Avery type up the notes. I was meticulous about keeping every e-mail, transcribed notes from every meeting, phone calls, and occasionally I would record random conversations in the elevator or during a meal with my cell phone without the other person knowing. Detail oriented—absolutely. And it helped me cover my ass.

By eight, I hung up the phone and heard Avery rustling outside my office door. Momentarily I looked at my inbox, wishing it would magically clean itself out. No time to worry about that now. I opened the door. "Good morning, Avery. Shall we get to it?"

Avery flashed her million-dollar smile. "Let's."

"First things first, can I borrow your chargers?" I held up my phones. "And can you order me new ones? I nearly lost my mind last night—not being connected."

AROUND SEVEN THAT night, I walked into my empty hotel suite and plunked down on the couch. I started to call out Sinclair's name, but then remembered that he had passed away and I was now living in a hotel. The company wasn't sure how long I would be stationed in Denver. The hope was only a couple of years if the doors didn't close in January. Cora called this a stepping-stone to the top. I had decided to keep my place in New York in case I was called back home sooner rather than later, and Beale Media would rent or buy a small house for me. A coworker who left her husband the same day I heard about my transfer ended up moving into my apartment. Since I moved so quickly, I hadn't had the time to start house hunting yet and didn't plan to for the first couple of weeks. Downtown Denver didn't appeal to me. Since I was in the same state as my parents after being gone for so long, it made sense for me to be closer to them. I just had to convince Cora.

I wasn't keen on spending too much time in Colorado. After living abroad and then in New York and several other cities, I feared I'd feel stifled in the West. Not that Denver was a forgotten wasteland. Cora had sent me to much smaller places before. There were too many memories in Denver, and I wasn't sure if I welcomed them yet. Or if I could handle them.

I thought of Claire. What did she do for fun?

Spent time with her husband and son, probably.

I frowned. I had constantly thought about Claire since landing at the airport, even though it had taken years to accept that Claire was gone for good.

And now I had to see her every day.

It felt like a gaping wound had been ripped opened for all to see. It nearly killed me the first time. Actually, I didn't think I ever got over her.

How was I going to get through the next two years, working side by side with her? That was, if I met corporate's demand by New Year's.

I groaned.

I thought back to our last night together. To the words Claire said and the unsaid accusation that Claire thought I wouldn't amount to anything and that Andrew was a safe bet. A provider.

Now I was the publisher of the paper Claire worked for. Did that impress her?

Did it matter? I rubbed my eyes and then massaged my temples.

She had a kid and was more than likely married.

I sighed while remembering the phrase, "You can never go home again."

"Shit," I muttered and walked to the minibar. The whiskey bottle practically called my name. My fingers reached out for the bottle that towered over the rest, and I remembered Claire asking me if anyone ever called me Dr. J, the six-foot-seven basketball star, the night we met at our dorm floor initiation meeting back in the first year of college. A lot of people teased me about my short stature, but when Claire made jokes about it, it didn't feel derogatory, but sweet somehow right from the start. Smiling, my fingers searched for and found some tonic water.

Ten years, now. I'd been clean and sober for ten years. Yet I still had to fight the urge on a regular basis.

I became quite adept at hiding my drinking and drug problem back in the day. Those in the know joked that I was a "high-functioning" addict. Amazingly enough, my addictions hadn't interfered with my job.

At first.

I could drink well into the early morning hours. To get through the day, I'd snort coke. I convinced myself that if I didn't start drinking until after work hours, I didn't have a problem. And on occasion I would go for a few days without either booze or drugs, just to prove to myself that I could. Ergo, I didn't have a problem.

For the most part, this logic had worked.

Then the cravings increased. My hands shook. I would break into a sweat during meetings. I was green around the gills or a sickly gray color. Cora, who grew up with an addict, recognized the signs. After years of managing it, I was on the brink of losing my career. I wasn't sure if that was a bad thing, but it was all I had. If I woke up with nothing to do, no job, no partner, no children, I feared I wouldn't make it. I'd go crazy. Or worse.

Cora recommended a program. I wasn't exactly thrilled about rehab and didn't think it would work.

The first time didn't.

Then I was busted for drunk driving. Normally I didn't have to worry about driving drunk since I lived in New York City. I could get plowed and then hail a cab. During a visit to Delaware, I got arrested the night before my friend's wedding. Not only did I miss the wedding, but I spent the night in the drunk tank. When I woke up, reality hit hard.

Again I turned to Cora, the only person I could trust. I used vacation time that I had accrued over a couple of years and went back to rehab. Everyone at work thought I was on the French Riviera, working on a novel. That was the cover story Cora circulated around the office.

When I returned to work, I looked healthy, without the Riviera tan. No one asked about the book that I was supposedly writing. That was when I realized my big secret wasn't such a secret. How long had my coworkers suspected? The thought was embarrassing, but I learned not to dwell on the past. Only think about the now. Too bad I couldn't stay off the shit.

Back in school, Claire used to tease me that I was an alcoholic in the making. And she always hated that after a bender she would be hungover and I would get up bright and early and go for a run or a bike ride.

God, if Claire knew …

I clutched the tiny tonic bottle, taking a massive swig, downing most of it with one gulp. I wiped my mouth with the back of my hand and decided to go to the hotel gym and run on the treadmill for an hour. Dull my mind that way so I wouldn't think about what happened that weekend. The weekend that spurred the Miracle Girl label that everyone loved but I loathed.

chapter three

After my first full week in the office, I stood in the break room with a handful of enraptured employees. I was telling my story about the night I had been camping with a photographer in Yellowstone and a bear tried tearing a hole in the side of my tent.

"What did you do?" asked Brenda, who always happened to be in the break room whenever I popped in to say hello to the troops.

"I panicked. I grabbed the nearest thing I could, which turned out to be my flashlight, and I bonked him on the head." I mimicked hitting the bear with my coffee cup.

"No way," said John, the director of classifieds.

"I know. It was stupid," I replied. "Like throwing oil onto a fire. But I was lucky. I think I stunned the bear enough by my idiocy, and he lumbered off, growling like he was getting his bear posse to come back and tear me limb from limb." I smiled sheepishly. I hated this story. Why did I keep telling it? Because people expected it of the Miracle Girl. Cora kept reminding me to bolster this image even though I hated it.

"Was it a grizzly?" asked John.

I shrugged. "I wasn't about to go out and introduce myself, John. Even though I grew up in Colorado, living in New York has turned me into a city girl."

"Then what happened?" Brenda whispered, barely breathing. It was hard for me not to stare at her crazy, frizzy hair. Was she intentionally going for the mad scientist look?

Many of them, eyes wide and mouths dangling open, waited for my response.

"Nothing. I fell asleep once my adrenalin crashed. The next morning, I woke up wondering if I had dreamt the whole thing. My photographer slept through the entire episode, so surely it didn't happen, right?"

"Did you? Dream it?" asked John with a knowing smile. It had to be a dream. How many people survived whacking a bear on the head with a flashlight?

I paused dramatically, sensing no matter what I said, they would believe me. "I was convinced I had. That it was just a dream. Then I went outside my tent to start a fire to make coffee, and I saw it." Again I stalled just a moment like I was on a Broadway stage. "Claw marks snagged all the way down the side of my tent." My voice was barely above a whisper, like I was reliving the feeling of dread.

Brenda gasped. With misty eyes, she pointed to her arm. "I get goose bumps just listening to your stories. What an exciting life you've led."

"I just go where the company sends me, but I do have to admit, I was glad when they transferred me to safer tasks, like running a paper." I winked at her.

"Is that why they call you the Miracle Girl?" asked John. He made quote marks with his stubby fingers.

I flinched when I heard the moniker, even though I had been expecting it. Not wanting to let on about my true feelings, I smiled awkwardly. "Maybe, John. But if I tell you the truth, I'll have to kill you. Company policy." God, did they think I was an idiot? I certainly did. However, I wouldn't put it past Cora to kill someone to keep the truth quiet.

Everyone chuckled and realized it was time to get back to work. Saying their good-byes, each one vacated the break room and headed back to their cubbies, where they spent the majority of their lives. The awake hours, at least.

Claire strolled in with a half-empty coffee cup. I smiled when I saw "World's Best Mom" scrawled on it in a child's handwriting. Back in school, not many saw Claire's soft side. She never desired attention. She left that to me. However, it was the little things that I loved about her, such as her never taking off her matching friendship bracelet for three years. Not until that night.

I noticed Claire trying to stifle a laugh while refilling her mug.

"What's so funny?" I asked, crossing my arms and leaning against the counter.

Claire turned, stirring some creamer into her drink. "Nothing." Her nothing wasn't convincing.

"I think I know you well enough to know when you're lying, Claire Nicholls." I loved that she had kept her maiden name.

"You always were a good storyteller."

"How long did you stand outside the door eavesdropping?" I uncrossed my arms and waggled an accusatory finger at her, amused by the smirk on her face.

"Long enough. Actually, it was hard not to finish the story for you."

I cocked my head, unsure. "What do you mean?"

"You've been telling that story for years. Except back then, it was your grandmother in the tent, not you." Claire burst into laughter.

I was confident that crimson spots dotted my cheeks and forehead.

Claire motioned to my face. "I'll make you a deal. I won't tattle as long as you buy me lunch today. I forgot mine." She shrugged as if it was a perfectly reasonable explanation for blackmail.

My broad smile sealed the deal.

"Did you even have an assignment in Yellowstone?"

"Yes, and my readers loved the bear part. Even my grandmother." I smirked.

"And what happens when people push you for details, like did you secure your food not to attract the bear?"

"Oh, I'm good at dancing around the details." I smiled confidently.

"I'm sure." Claire casually looked over her shoulder while walking out of the room and said, "I'll see you later, Miracle Girl." She made a gun with her fingers and pretended to shoot me.

"ARE YOU AVAILABLE at one?" I spoke into the phone.

I could hear Claire rustling some papers on her desk. "What?" A coworker said something unintelligible. "What's at one?"

I felt somewhat sick that she didn't remember our lunch date, but I pretended I wasn't stung by her forgetfulness.

"Lunch," I stated trying not to sound perturbed.

"JJ?"

I laughed, relieved. "Yes. Who'd you think I was?"

I heard her pen scratching on paper and imagined her signing some documents for an employee. The click of the door told me that Claire was alone. "Brenda. She's usually the only one who calls without identifying who it is. Most people stop by my office if they want something."

"I'm making a mental note of that. Don't call Claire. Stop by her office to ask her to lunch."

Claire giggled. "I'm pretty sure the publisher of the paper doesn't have to come crawling to my office if she wants something." Her tone was playful, like she and I had never ceased being friends.

"Oh, no. I wouldn't want to break tradition or step on Brenda's toes." I hung up.

Two minutes later I knocked quietly on Claire's door.

"Come in," said Claire. I entered and could tell she was deep in thought. She stood facing the back wall where she scrutinized ads for tomorrow's paper that hung on the corkboard behind her desk. Rather than rush to see who was disturbing her, she finished marking up the ads with a red pen. A delete sign here, followed by a corrected spelling of one word, and then she asked for the artwork to be centered on another. Clicking the cap onto her red pen, Claire finally turned to see me standing there, eyeing her.

"How in the hell did you get here so quickly?"

"I ran down the backstairs. Elevators are for wusses. Will one work for you, Claire Nicholls?"

Claire glanced at her watch. "It's one now."

"Then we better get going." I flashed my schoolgirl grin that had always made Claire smile. Her grin suggested it still worked like a charm.

"You haven't changed much," Claire announced before picking up her phone. "I'm going to lunch … Yes … I'll have my cell … 'Kay, put her on … How in the hell did that happen? … Okay, talk to the reps … All right, what do you want?" Claire grabbed her red pen again and scribbled some illegible words on her notepad. "See you soon."

"Anything I should be concerned about?" I asked, since it sounded important.

Claire let out a long breath. "We have too many full-page colored ads for this Saturday's paper. Talia just crunched the numbers and is at my assistant's desk, complaining."

I quirked an eyebrow.

"We ran a sale for full-page ads, and our reps didn't pay attention to the fact that we only had so many spots for each day. Talia, the diagrammer, is pulling her hair out." Claire laughed. "But she does that every day. She's a bit high-strung but damn good at her job, so we put up with her hissy fits."

"If we need to postpone—"

"Oh no. Trust me, Talia will have this settled in five minutes. Most of the sales reps are scared of her, and they want to stay on Talia's good side since she decides where every single ad is placed in the paper each day. She knows she holds the power. Some of the reps try to bribe her, but Talia is too high and mighty." Claire peeked out her door to see if anyone was listening. "When I was diagrammer, I never had to buy any scotch." She winked. Claire ripped off the note from the pad, stuffed it in her purse, and then stood and put her jacket on all in one motion. "I did say we'd stop off to buy her lunch. Poor thing never really gets to take a lunch break and the girl has a voracious appetite. You wouldn't know it by looking at her. Thin as a rail."

I motioned for Claire to walk ahead of me. In the parking lot, I pointed to my rental car.

"Are you kidding me? You were a bad driver in college. I can't even imagine how bad you are now after driving in the Big Apple and London. Do you remember the time you took out that fence? That rancher was pissed. He chased us on foot for over a mile."

"Hey, it was snowing."

"No, it wasn't. That's the story you've probably been telling since. Or was a bear chasing you?" She squeezed my arm. "Come on."

Claire strode to her Prius and hit the button on her key ring to unlock the doors.

"What are you in the mood for?" I asked as I crammed my short legs into the crowded space in the front seat, thankful that Claire hadn't changed all that much since school. No one would associate tidiness with her. Several newspapers and magazines were strewn about. Did she study the ads at red lights?

"Italian."

"I should have known." Back then, whenever we went out to eat, Claire always begged to go to Olive Garden. I gave in each and every time, even though I wasn't a fan. "Have they changed the menu at all?"

Claire peered at me out of the corner of her eyes. "You haven't been to the Olive Garden at all since school?"

I shook my head. I was a lot like my folks who preferred Mom and Pop establishments.

"Then it won't matter. It'll be new to you." She perked up in her seat.

"So that's a no."

Even the décor hadn't changed much inside. The only difference I noticed was that they no longer had an option for us to sit in a smoking section. I had been a heavy smoker. Claire the goody-goody only smoked occasionally when stressed or tipsy. I would suck down half a pack during one of our marathon dinners. Claire hammered down as much soup and salad as she could fit into her five-foot-seven frame. This used to make me jealous since I was inches shorter.

"Do you still smoke?" asked Claire, like she had read my mind.

"Occasionally, but I try not to." I fiddled with the salt shaker, accidentally spilling it.

"Quick! Throw it over your shoulder."

I chuckled, remembering Claire's silly superstitions, but I did as instructed.

"Not that shoulder. Your left!" Distraught, Claire crossed herself and said a silent prayer.

"Is the salt thing a Catholic superstition? And when did you convert?" I scrunched my forehead, shocked by her behavior.

Claire clearly had no answer to the first question and ignored it. "No, I didn't convert. It just—"

"Seemed like the right thing to do," I cut in, smiling.

The waitress saved Claire from any further explanation. We both ordered the all-you-can-eat soup and salad. Claire said she did for old time's sake, and I did since nothing else on the menu tempted me. It's hard to go wrong with soup and salad.

"It's nice to get away from the office, even if we are only a few blocks away."

"You don't go out to lunch that often?" I asked.

She shook her head. "Who has the time? Usually I eat at my desk, unless I have a business lunch, and those aren't relaxing." She flushed and then added, "You look good, JJ." Claire seemed unsure if she should say it.

"Thanks. You too. How long have you been working at the paper?" I took off my blazer and hung it over the back of my chair.

"Almost twenty years now. Feels like a hundred, though." Claire looked out the window and watched the hustle and bustle along the street.

"I like your coffee cup."

Claire snapped her head back and stared at me incredulously like I was making some inappropriate innuendo. "Excuse me?"

Knowing I sounded like an ass, heat rushed to my cheeks, causing a prickly sensation. "The cup in the office. Did your son make it for you?"

"Oh, that. I thought you were talking in some kind of code." Claire laughed over her suspicious mind. "I watch too many crime and spy movies."

"Do you still watch thrillers through the cracks of your fingers?"

Her embarrassed smile answered me. "Yes, and Ian made me that cup for Mother's Day."

"What's Ian like?"

I saw the tension leave Claire's shoulders. "Oh, he's a sweetheart. Just the other day he said he saw a butterfly on the TV and it made him think of me since it danced around the flowers. That's one of our things. We love to dance. Ian loves the oldies. You should see him reenact Elvis's hip movements. He can even do the famous lip snarl." Claire smiled fondly. A dark cloud descended in her eyes. "His father …"

It was only a matter of time until her husband came up. The one who gave Claire everything she ever wanted, including Ian.

"His father what?" I pushed, even though it was the last thing I wanted to discuss. I did, though, sense trouble on the home front. I felt scummy for pushing this, but I needed to know. Did I have a chance?

"Nothing. I'll be right back. I need to use the restroom."

I nodded, and when Claire was out of sight I pulled my Blackberry out of the pocket of my blazer to check e-mail in an effort to distract myself from dwelling on her marriage. I had failed miserably at getting the scoop. Was I contemplating being the other woman? No, I wouldn't, would I?

Sighing, I concentrated on my phone. Normally I had my Blackberry in sight at all times. But I knew my opportunities to be alone with Claire would be few and far between.

"Ah, you have a Crackberry." Claire slipped back into her seat effortlessly, and I admired how all of her movements flowed liked water even at our age. One had to look closely to see the action. My body was starting to show its age, and the aches and pains were building up daily. She continued, "They tried to get me one a few years back, but I put my foot down." It was Claire's turn to blush. "Not that I'm not dedicated to my job. People can reach me on my personal cell."

I slipped mine back into my pocket. "I'll requisition one for you when we get back." I leveled my gaze on Claire.

She sat utterly still.

"Geez, just kidding. I forgot you take everything at face value. Don't tell anyone, but there are quite a few people who have company phones who don't need them."

"It's going to cause a mini-riot if you start taking their phones away." Claire wasn't kidding.

"I know. But those are the cuts I want to make. Not jobs." I realized I was gritting my teeth, and the tightness in my shoulders and neck intensified. Just thinking about the consequences of failing turned me into a stress ball. "Let's not talk about work, though. We'll have plenty of time to do that."

"So, is the lion and the bath story true?" Claire grinned.

"You eavesdropped on that one as well?"

"Eavesdropped? Please! You told the story during an all-staff meeting. You'll soon find there's no privacy at all in our building. Everyone, and I do mean everyone, is into everyone else's business."

I had already suspected this. Fear caused people to circle the wagons. And most of the staff had been at the paper for years. It was one big apprehensive family.

"Yes. That story was true. I wish you could have been …" Flustered, I paused and then looked relieved when the waitress set down the salad bowl. I had always dreamed that we'd see the world together.

"Would you like grated cheese on top?" asked the woman.

Claire nodded enthusiastically.

When the woman left, Claire said, "I do believe that woman has saved both of us now."

"I've always liked your frankness. Glad to see that hasn't changed."

"What has changed about me?"

I flinched, not expecting her to put me on the spot, and I was slightly upset that I left myself wide open. Cora had trained me better and, even though this wasn't a business lunch, I was pretty sure if Cora was here she would have whacked the back of my head, muttering, "Idiot."

"N-nothing," I stuttered.

"Then why did you say it like that. 'Glad to see *that* hasn't changed' meaning something has changed." She was enjoying this.

"I don't believe I emphasized the word *that*," I stalled, knowing it wouldn't work. I focused on twisting the dark green napkin around my hand and smiled as I imagined a noose tightening around my neck.

Claire didn't speak, but she had a way of forcing me to speak with just a glare.

"Okay, okay. For one, you have a child now. That's a big change."

"And?" Claire prodded.

"You work in advertising, even though you swore up and down that you never would. I remember when I told you my father lined up a job for me in advertising and … well, you made it clear you thought I was settling. Selling out, even."

The hurt in Claire's false smile made me wince. I shouldn't have said that.

Claire shrugged it off. "Life happened." She tore off a piece of breadstick. "What about you? You're the big cheese now. What happened to my idealist who'd never wear a suit and wouldn't answer to *the man*?" She made quotation marks to the best of her ability since she was holding chunks of breadstick in each hand. "You wanted to be like Upton Sinclair." She smiled before popping some of the bread into her mouth and chewing menacingly.

"Same here. Life." My words sounded heavy with regret and disappointment.

She nodded knowingly and was silent for a moment. "College really didn't prepare us for the real world, did it?" Claire's eyes softened once again.

I laughed. "Not one bit."

"What brought you back to Denver? Was it just for work?"

I wasn't sure how to answer this question, and I sensed a lot depended on my response. "I've always wanted to come back, but work never allowed for it." This was partly true. Work always demanded a lot, yet I usually sought out work opportunities to keep me busy. "I didn't find out about this role until a week prior to boarding a plane."

Claire whistled. "Wow. Is it always like that?"

"Yes. I go where they send me."

"You always had one foot out the door, even back then." She smiled, but it didn't take the sting out of her words.

"Ah, yes. But this time, they want me to stay."

"Do you?"

"It depends, really."

"On what?"

"What I find here."

She tilted her head, inquisitive about what I meant, but she seemed hesitant to push. Would I be honest if she did?

chapter four

"Hello!" I shouted, after entering my parents' home.

"In the front room," Pops hollered back.

Pops had called and said if I didn't come over for dinner, Mom would hunt me down, lasso me, and drag me home. I'd been in town for a couple of weeks and besides meeting them for dinner my first night back, I hadn't seen them. They wanted their daughter back now that we were living in the same state.

Family dinners in my home were laid-back affairs. My dad usually would be sitting in front of the television watching sports. This hadn't changed since his retirement as a sportswriter. Three TV trays were set up, and Mom was already bringing the plates out. She knew I would be right on time.

"Who's playing?" I kissed Mom on the cheek before she scurried back to grab the rest. I would have offered to help, but she would just shush me. She was the uber-mom taking care of Pops and me, and her seventy-one years had been kind to her.

"The Nuggs versus the Jazz."

I took my seat. Try as I might, I could never get into sports. My father had taken me to games until he realized that I didn't enjoy them. I never told him, but he told me years later that during a Broncos game I spent more time chatting with the fans and workers than watching the game. "It was like you were conducting interviews on how people related to sports and why they went to a game in the middle of November," he had said. I didn't remember the incident, but he beamed when he relayed it. "I knew then that newspapers were in your blood. Not sports."

The newspaper line was one of his favorites that he repeated whenever the opportunity arose.

Mom rushed into the room with her plate. "Let's eat."

Mom and I talked, while Pops watched the game. He still dribbled food onto the front of his shirt on occasion, since his eyes were glued to the action, not on eating. Mom still chatted about her friends, the children and grandchildren of her friends, and movies she and Pops saw. Every Friday night, ever since I could remember, they went to the movies. No matter what.

It was always easy being around them. Quiet, simple, and loving. I longed for a relationship like theirs, but it eluded me. While they were content, I was always in action. Always wanting more. Pushing.

The game ended, and Pops and I headed to the kitchen. Ever since I could remember, we were in charge of dishes. I always washed, and he dried. They had a dishwasher, but Mom didn't like us using it. I think it was her way of getting us together. My father was pretty quiet, and I was always going Mach speed. Doing dishes each night forced us to have a daily conversation.

"Make sure you don't leave dry chunks," Mom yelled. "I'll make you do them again."

Once, Pops and I came up with a plan for her to allow us to use the dishwasher. We intentionally did a crappy job. Mom saw through our ploy and woke us both up in the middle of the night to redo all the dishes. It was the first and last time we tried getting out of our nightly chore.

"She still hasn't forgotten," I mumbled.

"Memory of an elephant. I can't get away with anything." He blushed at the thought.

I wondered what my sweet father would try to get away with. He didn't drink, smoke, or cheat. As far as I knew, he had never been pulled over for a speeding ticket or ever received a parking fine. Neither had my mom. God, they would cringe if they knew all the stuff I had done. I was honest with my parents to a point.

With towel in hand, Pops asked, "How's the paper?"

I groaned. The warm water in the sink felt good. Scrubbing a plate, I said, "I'm not sure I can save it."

He grunted. "It's a shame. I know you'll do your best." I looked over my shoulder and saw his eyes were misty. "I have so many fond memories working there."

"I want to save it, Pops."

He stopped drying the plate and eyed me with his sincere look. "I know, sweetheart. And if anyone can, you can."

I waited for the dreaded Miracle Girl label, bracing for my reaction. Instead he said, "Newspapers are in your blood."

I laughed. "How do I infect the rest of Colorado?"

"Easy. Bite them!" He mimicked a vicious dog.

"I hear too much talking, not enough washing," said my mother. "Hurry up. I want to go out for pie."

That got our attention. There was a diner around the corner they'd been frequenting for over four decades.

Dinner in front of the television and then pie at the local diner. So simple and satisfying. Why did I complicate the hell out of my life?

"Sounds good, Mom. We should be done in a jiffy."

chapter five

It was Friday night and I, per usual, didn't have any plans. My parents invited me to a movie, but I knew that Fridays were their date night and didn't want to intrude. Also, I didn't want to admit that I had no plans. They worried about me being alone.

Massaging my temples in hopes of easing the pain, I realized I was a bore. Here I was on a Friday night, having a glass of ice water on the balcony of a five-star hotel, brooding about what used to be.

Staring at my empty hotel room, I thought back to the days when I always had plans. A time when I barely slept alone. But those days, when I woke the next morning, there was a good chance I didn't know the woman's name or it was a woman I swore I would never sleep with again. Each morning I rushed the woman out of my apartment, cursing myself for being so stupid yet again. The drugs and alcohol had played a large part, but I think the biggest issue was my fear of being alone. I hated being alone. It scared the crap out of me.

These days I felt alone, even when among others. I was back then as well, but now I appreciated the feeling. I had to learn to like myself, and that wasn't an easy task.

Right after I kicked the booze and coke, I still had a hard time admitting I was an addict and that I needed to cut most of my ties. I tried going to parties sober, but not many want a sober person at a party. I didn't quit my friends; they quit me. Women no longer wanted to stay the night.

Outside of work, I didn't matter to anyone anymore. I knew my employees had to listen to my stories, the true and made-up ones. They had to ooh and ahh in all the right places. Some of the oohs and ahhs may have been real, but that didn't matter. I still craved that feeling. Even if most of it was all pretend.

I sighed heavily, knowing I still yearned for it. I needed to stop it, but I wasn't sure how. I was the Miracle Girl with all the amazing travel stories. On one hand, the image helped me foster relationships with people at work since it was an automatic conversation starter. On the other, I was using them to feed my need, and since moving back to Denver, the need was growing. The void I was always so desperate to fill was growing at an exponential and alarming rate. This terrified me.

My watch read 9:00 p.m. That was late enough to go to bed. Before tucking in for the night, I requested a 6:00 a.m. wake-up call so I could go for a run before heading into work on a Saturday. The higher-ups admired my work ethic and loved that I worked six to seven days a week. Most didn't know I did that to stay sober.

Not that I would ever really admit that completely, I thought. I convinced myself ninety percent of the time that I loved my job.

That was the only thing that made me feel happy.

Complete.

My life was built on lies. When would it all come crashing down?

"SHIT," I MUTTERED when I opened my eyes the following morning. As soon as I woke, I knew it was going to be a bad day.

It was nearly impossible to lift my head off the pillow without excruciating pain. Every so often, usually during stressful times, my neck paralyzed me. Not only was the soreness unbearable, but it became so stiff and heavy it felt like my shoulders fused into the bottom of my skull during the night, leaving my upper body with little to no mobility.

Slowly I eased off the bed and carefully walked to where my purse sat on the desk by the window. I cradled my neck with one hand, holding it firmly so it wouldn't snap in half. Not that it could, but it felt like a stiff twig that would crack with any sudden movement, no matter how slight.

The sun hadn't appeared over the horizon yet, but daylight was already stretching its fingers across the landscape. I rummaged through my bag, looking for Advil.

"Fuck!" Failing to find my emergency stash, I suddenly remembered taking the pills out of my bag at work yesterday, and I didn't remember putting them back in my purse. The nagging headache I had all day yesterday was a warning sign that my neck was about to go on strike. I should have seen this coming and should have been prepared. *Great, just great, JJ,* I cursed my carelessness.

Ignoring the stiffness wasn't possible. I looked down at my PJs—a T-shirt and boxers. I would have to put on a pair of jeans, but I said no to wearing a bra. I wasn't that large, and odds were no one would notice the girls jiggling around. This thought made me smile since they didn't jiggle all that much even when unfettered.

I eased back onto the bed and tried to wrangle a pair of jeans on to no avail. My arms weren't long enough, and I couldn't bend my upper body. After a short rest, I stood and held the jeans in front of me. After several failed attempts, I managed to get one leg in. Again I needed to take a break. Standing there with one leg in, I felt like the world's worst mime mimicking getting dressed in Central Park.

Taking a deep breath, I got the left leg in. The simple act of getting dressed was exhausting, and my sweaty T-shirt clung to my body to reveal I wasn't wearing a bra. But the thought of lifting my shirt off, putting on a bra, and then replacing my shirt made me cringe. Instead, I yanked a scarf off the desk to conceal my erect nipples and threw a jacket over my shoulders. I grabbed my wallet out of my purse, knowing I wouldn't be able to sling the purse over my shoulders, and marched out of the hotel room, resembling Frankenstein. The grimaces and low moans I couldn't stop added to the effect.

At Walgreens, three blocks from the hotel, I stocked up on Advil and Bengay. For some reason, this store placed all the heating pads on the top shelf. I was barely above five foot three, and even on my best days I always struggled reaching the top shelf in most stores. Briefly, I considered not trying. There was no way I would ask a clerk for help. I never liked to ask for help.

But I knew the pad would ease the pain. Holding my neck with one hand to stabilize it as much as possible, I extended my other arm slowly, likely resembling a drunk person reaching for something that didn't exist.

"JJ?" Footsteps came closer. "Are you okay?"

I lowered my arm and slowly turned my entire body to face Claire. I smiled shyly, knowing I was busted. "Yeah, I just—"

"What's wrong with you?" Claire interrupted. "You're standing funny. Why are you holding your neck like that? Are you drunk?" She whispered the last question and looked around nervously like police officers would rush in and arrest us both.

Even though the action hurt like hell, I couldn't stifle the laughter that forced its way out. "You never could wait for an answer and always jumped to conclusions."

Claire smiled bashfully, turning pink. "I'm sorry."

"Why are you here so early?"

"I popped in here before going to the office to take care of some stuff." She waved a hand in the direction of the office, which was one block away. "Now, will you tell me what's wrong?"

I still held my neck while massaging the pain away from laughing. "It's my neck. It's … well, it's hard to explain really. I get this pain—"

"You always were a pain in the neck," Claire butted in again.

I started shaking my head at the joke and winced. "Are you going to mock me or help me?"

"Yes, of course. I'm sorry. What are you trying to reach, Dr. J?" Claire's face didn't show any trace that she just called me the nickname she'd given me in college the first time we met. She hadn't been the first to mock my stature, but she had been the first to do so in a way that didn't feel insulting. Instead it had created an instant bond. I always thought after we became close friends, when she called me Dr. J it was the closest she ever came to saying I love you. And using the nickname in Walgreens felt like it erased the twenty-odd years we'd been apart and like we'd never said good-bye.

Snapping back to reality, I pointed to the heating pad. "That, my Jolly Green Giant."

Claire's eyes settled onto mine for a brief second, and I thought she was going to reach out and touch my cheek. Instead, she reached for the heating pad. "No one has called me the Jolly Green Giant—"

"Since school?" I wanted to say "since me" but didn't feel bold enough. Claire wasn't that much taller, but when you were only five-three, everyone seemed like a giant.

"Here," Claire motioned to the small basket near my feet. "Let me carry this for you. Do you need anything else?"

I wanted to shout, "You. I need you! I've always wanted you." Instead I uttered a weak no.

Claire walked me to the front of the store.

"Wait," I said, motioning to her empty hands with my free hand. "Don't you need anything?"

Claire's face shot up in flames. "Uh … it's okay. I'll come back later."

I turned and marched for the aisle I was certain Claire needed. Momentarily, the pain in my body had ceased. Claire followed reluctantly.

I pointed to the maxi pads. "You never could talk about anything private."

"Oh, you think you know me so well, do you?" Claire's eyes showed she was teasing. "I no longer use these, but these." Claire pulled a box of tampons off the shelf.

"Really? You finally graduated?" All throughout college, Claire rejected the idea of tampons. She thought them undignified—sticking something inside her. I never could wrap my head around her stubbornness and couldn't fathom why a grown woman would want to wear a bloody diaper. That seemed undignified to me.

She wandered to the aspirin aisle and grabbed a box of children's aspirin. "This is the real reason I'm here. I have a feeling Ian will need some after this weekend. Come on, Dr. J."

We each paid for our things and left the store.

In the parking lot, Claire pointed to her Prius. "Do you need a lift to your hotel?"

"Thanks, but it's a short walk from here."

Claire nodded, but I sensed a bit of disappointment.

"Would you like to go to breakfast? It's the least I can do after you rescued me." Then I remembered. "Or do you need to get back home to Ian…?"

"Oh no, Ian and his father are skiing today. Or attempting to, I imagine." She smiled. "That's why I'm up so early. I had to drop … them off." Claire looked flustered.

I was sure she was lying, but why lie about her son and husband going skiing? And where had she dropped them off? It was an hour and a half drive to the nearest slopes.

"Breakfast would be lovely," she said after a moment's hesitation.

"Is Olive Garden open this early?" I teased.

Claire swatted my arm and immediately regretted it. "Oh, did I hurt your neck?"

"Not one bit." Nothing at that moment could hurt me. I felt ten feet tall and bulletproof with her standing next to me.

"Good. Let's take my car since it's here. Not only are you a bad driver, but how can you check your blind spot if you can't turn your neck." Her demeanor showed she wasn't looking solely for an excuse to take her car. She truly was alarmed by my inability to check my blind spot. Oh, if she only knew.

I wanted to kiss her. How was I, the tainted Miracle Girl, head over heels with such a do-gooder?

WE SAT AT a small table in a trendy breakfast place near my hotel. Claire crinkled her nose. "Really, you're getting green chili chicken hash?" she asked after we placed our orders.

"Yeah. Why?"

"It just seems a tad heavy this early."

"Because biscuits and gravy are a super-light snack." I winked at her.

Claire laughed over her mistake. "I forgot you like spicy food."

"And I forgot you can't handle pepper on a baked potato." I fidgeted in my chair. The pills were starting to take the edge off the pain, but the stiffness wasn't going away.

"You always did like to live on the edge. Any more bear stories I haven't heard?" Claire sipped her water, innocently batting her eyelashes.

"Nope. No more bear stories. Do you remember that time in Honduras when you were convinced you were being chased by a snake?" I laughed. We'd gone to Honduras over spring break our sophomore year with her church youth group to build houses. "I can still see you running down the dirt steps screaming, 'Kill him, JJ. Kill him!'"

"You didn't kill him."

"How could I? He slithered away so fast all I saw was a flash of his rainbow colors. He probably died of fright from all of your screaming." I guffawed. "There have been many days when I've replayed that moment in my head. The way you jumped over that boulder, and then had to come to a skidding halt to avoid going over a hundred-foot cliff, all the while your arms flailing about like you were trying to fly away." I shook my head. "All for a tiny, harmless snake."

"Harmless!"

I pinned her with a knowing look.

She smiled. "You should write adventure novels. Not manage a paper that's dying."

"Dying … that seems a bit dire." I tried to erase the agreement from my face.

"You think you can save it?"

I leveled my gaze and said with earnestness, "I'm going to do everything I can to save it."

"Good luck. Most of the staff doesn't realize that we need to build up an online presence. They think our customers are eagerly waiting by their doorsteps each morning to read the paper. To feel it in their hands. To make that crinkling sound when they turn the pages." She mimicked opening a paper and shaking it. "Say the word Twitter to them and they'll stare at you like you're speaking another language. They have no idea that most of our customers are getting old. Subscriptions are in the shitter. We can't rely on the paper. We need to broaden our online presence."

"Shitter!" I laughed. The Claire I knew never swore, but I had noticed she was quite comfortable cursing these days. Being around newspaper people had corrupted my Claire. Of course she had no idea how stained I had become over the years. I did my best to hide that from everyone.

"I'm scared. I have a child. I can't lose my job." Her voice cracked. "I watched the last team come in and wipe out half of the management jobs. One by one, someone would walk them out at the end of the day and tell them not to come back. They fired our top sales manager the day she signed a million-dollar account. It's messed up. It was that day when I realized none of our jobs were safe."

I wasn't sure how to respond. I knew all this, of course, and I knew the reasons behind it. That sales manager had been in cahoots with another paper and was trying to take all of her clients with her. I didn't agree with all the decisions corporate made, but I knew I couldn't divulge too much either. I was privy to information that Claire, or anyone at the Denver paper, wasn't, and I couldn't say that no one else would lose their job since I never made promises I couldn't keep.

"I'm sorry. I know the last guy who was here wasn't very popular."

Claire snorted. "That's an understatement."

I put a palm up. "Listen, we aren't looking to fire people at the moment."

"At the moment … but it's not off the table." She tugged at her napkin, angrily.

Claire's face was tense and frightened. I wanted to reassure her. "Claire, I can't make any promises, but I need you to trust me. I won't do anything to …" I almost blurted I would never hurt her. That I would never let the company fire her. Was that true? I wasn't the type to get involved personally when it came to work. That was one of the reasons they'd sent me here. I was an insider, yes, but not an impassioned one. But this was different. This was Claire.

My Claire.

Claire nodded her head like she understood the unspoken promise. "I'm glad you're back. I've missed you. You've always been able to talk me off the ledge." She let out a relieved sigh.

She was always a nervous Nellie. Every finals week she would be on edge and insisted that I spend every waking hour with her to help keep her tranquil. Some nights she would fall asleep in my bed, saying she couldn't sleep without my calming aura.

"What are you thinking about?" she asked.

"Finals week."

Claire blushed. "Oh, you were always so patient. I still remember when you sat outside my calculus final sending me positive thoughts. I swear to this day, that's the only reason I passed. You always believed in me."

I shifted in my seat, and she gulped her water. Neither of us mentioned that she hadn't believed in me that night. That last night.

The waitress arrived with our meals. "Here ya go."

Claire eyed the jalapenos on my plate. "I'm getting heartburn just looking at them."

I forked one and popped it into my mouth, chewing with gusto.

"You're crazy, JJ Cavendish."

You're beautiful, Claire, I thought. God, I wanted to scream this so everyone would know how much I loved the woman sitting across from me. Yet, I felt the tug of the past, and couldn't.

As we finished our meals, Claire motioned for the waitress to bring the check. I slouched back in my chair to relieve the pressure on my full gut, immediately regretting it when spasms of pain shot down the length of my body and back up to the original source. Instinctively, I cradled my neck.

"Do you remember when you conned me into taking that massage class with you?" Claire looked at me confidently.

I couldn't stop the grin from transforming my entire face into pure ecstasy. "Uh, I plead the fifth." I had begged her for days to take the class with me. It was my desperate attempt to get my hands on her body.

"Yeah, right. Even back then I knew why."

"What does that mean?" I leaned closer to the table, anxious for the answer, but unsure how I would handle the news.

"Oh, please. I knew from the moment we met that you liked me."

My laugh was loud and boisterous. "Liked you. My, my, my … you have a big head on your shoulders."

"Am I wrong?"

"Not one bit."

Claire reddened. "Well, I do remember some things I learned in that class …" Her voice broke, and she didn't complete her thought.

"And?" I expected Claire to say her husband benefitted greatly from it now. Or some dig along those lines.

Claire didn't respond, instead she pointed to me like that answered the question completely.

"Are you asking me if I remember what we learned? Yes, I do." Not that I'd had many opportunities to show off my massage skills lately. I hadn't been with a woman in three years. Wow—that was a depressing thought. After kicking my addictions, I'd stopped sleeping around so much. According to my therapist, that was another of my compulsions I had to deal with.

"No, you dope. Your neck. I can massage your neck for you."

Taken aback, I responded, "That's very kind of you, but …" But what? All words slipped out of my brain.

"Don't be silly. You're my boss, but we're still friends. At least I hope we're still friends." Claire's penetrating blue eyes were sensually low-lidded as she watched my reaction.

I nearly shouted, "My hotel is right around the corner. Let's leave the car. It'll be faster." Instead I said, "Of course we're still friends." I attempted to say her name without any meaning. I failed. I knew I spoke her name like a lover cherishing every letter.

A mysterious look crossed Claire's face, and I was certain I had blown my chance. Surely she was searching for the words to let me down easily and to say that maybe it wasn't a good idea after all. No way should the two of us be alone in my hotel room. I hadn't considered that Claire would invite me, her former lover, to her home. Not the home she shared with her son and husband. Only a hotel would suit the situation. Thinking this made me feel dirty, but not completely. Even after all these years I felt that I was meant to be with Claire. Claire was mine. Mine and mine alone.

"Great. Let's go," stated Claire as the waitress placed the bill on the table.

I snatched the bill and sashayed to the cashier, pulling my wallet out of my jeans pocket faster than a gunslinger in the Old West. I wasn't going to give Claire any time to consider what could possibly occur.

Sitting in Claire's car, I pondered what would happen. Maybe Claire was only being kind. I was obviously in pain, and Claire was always a goody-goody. A helper. It was only a neck rub. Nothing more. I kept chanting this in my head, not wanting to get my hopes up.

But the way Claire had looked at me when she opened the car door in the parking lot. The way she "accidentally" brushed her shoulder against me—that wasn't Claire the goody-goody. That was Claire on the prowl. It was a new side to her that I found fascinating, thrilling, and goddamn confusing.

Truth be known, I was praying this day would turn into more. Maybe not a roll in the hay, but a start. I wouldn't be able to hang on much longer without her. At first, when I accepted the job, I felt confident I could live in Colorado again with Claire. It was a big state. Not as populated as New York, but more land. It was big enough for the two of us to live separately. Hell, I didn't even think I'd run into Claire.

My Claire. Oh, how I wish I could say that out loud. My Claire.

Now I was in Claire's car and we were heading to the hotel where Claire was going to massage my neck. It had to mean something, didn't it? Or could fate be that cruel?

I remembered all of my tortured years. The years being her best friend and nothing more. And then that night. One night of bliss, before we were torn apart for what had seemed like an eternity.

Yes, fate could be a bitch. A fucking cunt.

I let out a long, anguished sigh.

Claire placed a hand on my thigh. "You okay? Is your neck that bad?"

Her touch caused a wave of emotion in my body. A longing that never died in the past twenty-five years. As much as I tried to numb myself, that desire boiled underneath. Now I had to control it with her hands on my bare skin. Shit, maybe this was a bad idea. A horrendous idea that would crash and burn.

I closed my eyes, focusing all of my strength on not placing my hand on Claire's, which still rested on my thigh, and letting Claire know just with one touch how insanely mad I was with love and desire. "Yeah, it's okay."

Claire didn't remove her hand. Sitting at a red light, I fought the desire to stare at the hand. Devour it with my eyes. Memorize all the lines, creases, and blemishes. I forced my head to the passenger window and stared.

Then I felt Claire's hand squeeze my leg. "We're here."

Speechless, I remained motionless.

"Here, let me help you out." Claire dashed to the passenger side, thinking I was paralyzed by my neck. There were spasms coursing through my body, but they emanated from my nether regions. I feared my panties were soaking wet, and Claire would see the effect she still had on me. And all just from the touch of her hand on my leg.

Fuck! I suddenly remembered I was wearing boxers. Of all the idiotic things! Why did I have to dress like a super-dyke today of all days? I never left the house in boxers. I only slept in them, but how could I explain that?

Claire leaned closer, and her rose perfume, the same scent from years ago, overwhelmed me. I wanted to bury my nose in her neck, to smell only Claire. To this day, I couldn't stand being near a rose. The memory of Claire was too intense. Being surrounded by roses every Valentine's Day in the office was brutal. Usually I would make up some excuse to work from home on February fourteenth.

"You sure you're okay? You seem stiffer now than when I first saw you this morning." Claire's concern was evident in the careful way she eased me out of the vehicle.

"I'm fine, I promise." I wanted to leave my arm around Claire's shoulders, but Claire was too tall by four bloody inches. Instead I was bold enough to wrap my arm around Claire's waist, careful not to hold her too suggestively.

We entered the hotel room, and Denver's famous thin air almost eluded me completely. I sucked in deeply, while Claire stared at the view.

"I don't know how you lived so far away from the mountains. I could never leave them." Claire spoke with her back to me.

I wanted to reach out, take Claire in my arms, and announce, "I don't know how I lived so far away from you."

Before I had a chance to say anything, Claire turned around crisply. "Okay, let's get your shirt off."

I shuffled back stiffly and fell onto the bed. "What?"

"How am I going to give you a massage if you have a shirt on?" Claire tapped her foot while wearing a silly grin that erased twenty years from her face.

"But, it's just my neck." I pointed to my bare neck to emphasize the point, kicking myself for doing so.

"No it's not. You can't move your upper body at all."

It was true, but I was seized with trepidation. How could I remove my shirt in front of Claire?

"Come on," said Claire as she strutted over to me in three steps.

"But … but I don't have a bra on. I couldn't get it on earlier," I explained completely aghast. I crossed my arms over my breasts protectively, unclear about what threat Claire posed to my tits.

Claire laughed. "JJ, you don't have anything I haven't seen before."

Heat rose to my face. Lamely I said, "I have a tattoo you haven't seen."

"Really?" Claire quirked one eyebrow. "Let me see it."

Let her see it. If I did that, Claire would know about my past. The alcohol. The drugs. Rehab. The Miracle Girl fraud. No. I couldn't let her see the tattoo I got after my third and final stint in rehab. No, I couldn't let Claire see that about me. She would never understand. Never forgive. She was too pure to understand how weak I had been.

But it was too late. Claire had forcefully, but still delicately enough not to hurt, lifted my shirt off and casually thrown it onto the floor. I stared at the crumpled shirt, wondering how that happened so quickly.

"Oh, it's beautiful." Claire's fingertips outlined the large koi fish on my lower back. I had to sit through two sessions to complete it. "What does it mean?"

"What?" I could barely force the question out, still eying my shirt.

"Koi. I remember it has a meaning, but I can't remember what." Claire continued to fondle the tattoo.

I told myself she's just fingering the tattoo, not me. "Perseverance in difficult times. Buddhists claim it symbolizes courage." Which at the moment, I felt I was completely lacking in that department.

"It seems alive, like it's ready to jump right off your back. Did it hurt?"

"A little. You get used to the pain … numb to it."

Claire sat on the bed next to me. "How should we do this?" She motioned to the bed.

I stood abruptly. "What do you mean?" I stuttered.

Claire stifled a laugh. "Can you lay down or do you want me to straddle you from behind … to rub your neck?"

"Oh, that. I think I can lie down." I didn't move. Claire patted the bed, prompting me to be a good patient.

She sat to the side, kneading my neck carefully. "Do you have any other tattoos?"

"Yes." I was hesitant to answer. Would Claire find that gaudy?

"How many?"

"One more. A tiny one on my ankle."

"What is it?"

"A word."

"What word?"

"Remember."

"You had the word remember tattooed on your body. What are you afraid of forgetting?"

Who I am? was my first thought. *What happened?* was my second. "Uh, it depends."

Claire dug in a little deeper, and I sucked in some breath.

"I'm sorry, did that hurt?"

"No, it felt really good actually."

"You should make an appointment with my chiropractor."

"Chiropractor? You see a chiropractor?" I tried to turn my head to see Claire's face. She had to be teasing.

"Yeah. Why is that so odd?" She gripped my flesh harder, like she knew it was what I wanted.

"Seems odd for you. Too experimental," I explained.

"Well this may shock you, JJ Cavendish, but I'm not the same girl you left behind. I even have an acupuncturist."

I started to sit up, shocked, but Claire held my body down on the bed. To keep me in place, she straddled me. "Does it hurt your neck if I sit here?" She leaned down to hear my answer, and I got a whiff of her perfume. All of a sudden, I had a desire to run through endless rows of rose bushes completely naked. Thorns and all. I wanted to feel everything.

"Not one bit." I felt Claire's warmth through her jeans, and it radiated through me.

"It's getting warm in here." Claire's cardigan plummeted to the carpet. "Are you hot?"

"A little," I admitted.

Claire's T-shirt billowed to the floor. I was tempted to see if she was only in a bra, but opted to wait.

"I always wear too many layers." Claire worked her way along my bare back, using both palms stroking downward.

"How many layers do you have left?" I asked with as much boldness as I could muster.

"Just one. Two, if you count my bra. I never leave home without one, but you can get away with it."

True. Claire's voluptuous breasts begged to be tamed by satin. I had used to try to convince Claire to go running with me, but she would always clutch at her breasts and say, "Not with these bazookas. I'd end up with black eyes."

"Doesn't seem fair. I'm half-naked, and you're fully clothed."

Claire slapped my back playfully.

My heart sank. The ploy didn't work, and I had to admit to myself that it was a pathetic attempt and way too obvious. No wonder she didn't fall for it.

Then I felt Claire's weight shift, and another shirt tumbled to the ground.

Claire leaned down and whispered in my ear, "Is that better?" I felt the softness of her bra on my skin.

"You're getting there." I held my breath, waiting to see her response.

"If you want more layers off, you'll have to take them off yourself." Claire's breath tickled my ear.

"Mine or yours?" I didn't know why I was being cagey. After all these years I felt like an idiot for tempting fate.

"Both."

I started to move.

"Not yet, I'm not done giving you a massage."

Claire sat up and resumed on my lower back. "What happened?"

Confused by the sudden change in Claire's tone, I asked, "When?"

"The tattoo … perseverance during adversity. What happened?"

I felt her fingers trace the outline of the tattoo. Did it take her this long to come up with the courage to ask about its meaning? Or had my other tattoo distracted her?

Claire's fingers worked right above the waistline of my jeans. I felt her tug on the waistline of my boxer shorts, but I didn't bother to explain why I was wearing them and she didn't say anything.

I was too focused on her question. I knew I should be honest, but not completely honest. "Things … life got a little …" I didn't know how to tell Claire. "I got the tattoo when I returned to New York City after a difficult … assignment." I stumbled over the word assignment, and I wondered if she knew I was lying. "I … well, I was lucky to be alive. To have survived."

I could sense Claire nodding her head. "It's okay. You can tell me."

"I did some things I shouldn't have. I have a lot of regrets. A lot."

"Me too," whispered Claire. "Me too." Silence flooded the room. "But I'm done having regrets. It's not worth it."

I expected her to get up, get dressed, and storm out of the room, muttering to herself that she was a fool to risk the life she had with Ian and his father. I waited for it to happen. For her to realize what she was about to do.

What I didn't expect was for Claire to lie down on top of me and hold me. "I should have trusted you back then. I know that now."

I felt Claire's skin against my own. Never before had I been completely overwhelmed by the simple act of touching. I let the feeling overtake me before rolling over, so I was now on top of Claire, staring into her face. Tenderly, I brushed some hair off her cheek, leaving my hand there. The pain and stiffness in my neck vanished.

Claire started to speak, but I silenced her by putting a finger on her lips. I ran my free hand down her bare skin. I could see and feel goose bumps exploding over her body like fireworks. It was only a matter of moments now before we kissed, and I wanted to relish the final seconds before we crossed the line. Relish the anticipation for a moment longer.

"I never stopped thinking about you," I said before I leaned down and brushed my lips against Claire's neck, taking in her scent. "I have replayed that one night in my head a thousand times, and each time I run after you. God, Claire, that's my biggest regret of all."

Claire made the move. She kissed me with an all-consuming fervor. I opened my mouth, and her tongue explored softly but determined. The need to be closer grew with each second. Both of us ripped off the other's remaining clothes. I couldn't control myself anymore. I had to be inside Claire. To be as close as I possibly could be. I thrust my finger inside, and her wetness welcomed me while Claire pulled my face back to hers and kissed me with a desire that I had never experienced. Not even that first and only time we had made love so many years ago. As we kissed, I continued thrusting my finger in as deep as I could and sensed Claire was close to coming. It was fast, but there was no way to slow down the emotions. Not after this long. All the wanting. Desire. Twenty-five years was coming to fruition.

Claire's body started to quiver, and I felt I was close to exploding myself. We came at the same moment, letting out a flood of pent up emotions. I collapsed onto Claire, breathing heavily. She ran her hand through my short hair.

"I'm sorry. I didn't mean to come so fast," said Claire.

I smiled. "Never apologize for that."

"It's just that … it's been so long …"

"Since we made love?"

"Since I've been with anyone," Claire confessed.

I propped my head up on my palm and traced a finger on Claire's chest. "Me too."

"How long?" she asked.

"Three years. You?"

"Longer."

I couldn't control my eyes from popping. I felt a sudden rush of cold air on them. "Longer? Really?" Had she and Ian's father divorced? Was that what she'd been doing this morning, dropping Ian off at his dad's? The question was on my lips, but I let it slip back inside. It wasn't time to tug on that thread.

She nodded and then smiled mischievously. "Shall we go again, but slower this time?"

I answered with a delicate and leisurely kiss.

Hours later, the sun hung low in the sky, slowly waving good-bye for the night, but promising to return the next day. Claire was leaning against the headboard, and I rested my head on her lap. I could smell Claire's juices, and the scent calmed me. It wasn't a dream. We had made love repeatedly.

"How's your neck?" asked Claire, and then she sniggered.

"Never felt better. Who knew this was the cure."

"I did of course."

"Is that why, then?" I teased.

"Maybe it was one of the reasons," Claire said in all seriousness.

I sat up. Claire's stern face slowly dissolved to show me she was pulling my chain.

"I'm starving." She padded to the desk, naked. She rifled through some takeout menus. Turning to me she asked, "Chinese?"

I nodded, afraid to ask the question I wanted to. How long until Claire had to return home? To Ian? I was fairly certain a husband wasn't in the picture anymore. Poor Claire. All she wanted was permanence, and it seemed that eluded her.

Claire sat on top of me before picking up the telephone on the bedside table. During the call, she flicked my nipple with a finger. When she hung up, I said, "Good Lord. You ordered enough food for an army."

"Are you complaining?" She placed her finger into my mouth. "I'm not done with you yet." To emphasize her point, she removed her finger and touched my clit before licking my juices off of her finger.

"Then you're staying … the night, I mean."

Claire nodded. "Ian doesn't get back until tomorrow night." A naughty smile broke across her face. "We have twenty minutes until the food arrives. Can you think of anything we can do for twenty minutes?"

"Jog in place."

"Don't try being cute. You're much better using your mouth in other ways."

CLAIRE LEFT THE following evening. I stood at the window, staring at the foothills, confused by my emotions. Her scent still lingered in the room. Closing my eyes, I imagined holding Claire in my arms while in actuality I clutched a shirt she'd left behind. There was a nagging thought in the back of my mind. Yesterday morning, Claire expressed she was terrified of losing her job. Did she … no, that couldn't be the reason. I blocked the thought from spoiling my memories of the weekend. I flipped open my laptop.

It was time for me to do what I did best. Plan. Tomorrow morning I had a meeting with all the heads of the departments to begin our last-ditch effort to save the paper. One thing was clear: circulation wasn't the answer.

From the numbers I saw, each month we lost subscribers, not gained. Advertising was stagnant. The paper was like a car running on fumes. I had to ignite a spark to keep the engine going full steam ahead.

I thought of one of my favorite Hearst quotes: *Putting out a newspaper without promotion is like winking at a girl in the dark—well-intentioned, but ineffective.*

chapter six

Everyone sat around the table, waiting for me to start the meeting. I looked each person in the eye, eleven in total, before stating the Hearst quote.

Everyone chuckled except for Darrell, the senior editor. I took in his appearance. He was fifty-three years old, according to his employment files. He wore a short-sleeve plaid shirt, tucked crisply into his khakis. It was apparent he took care of his body, but he didn't attempt to avoid taming his nerdy appearance. The man sported black-framed glasses that had been all the rage in the fifties. Some people today could pull them off. Darrell wasn't one of them.

I knew he would be the bane of my existence, resisting any and all change. I had to put my foot down immediately and make it clear to him and to the rest of the staff that I was in charge. Years earlier, Darrell had called all the shots. But then corporate had stepped in and demoted him back to news. Henry, the corporate guy before me, failed to get Darrell in line. I didn't intend to let that happen twice. Firing him right off the bat wasn't an option. What everyone in the room didn't know was that Darrell's time at the paper was almost up. I wanted the timing to be perfect, but right now he was a pawn. Harsh, yes, but necessary. My mentor taught me there was no such thing as being nice in this business. Go for the jugular, before the other person did.

This meeting was a way for me to let people know I was willing to listen to new ideas, but that my word was final. I was in charge. Not Darrell.

"What can you guys tell me about social media? What's hot? What's not? What are we using? What should we be using more effectively?"

I stared at a sea of blank faces. Claire's face was supportive, and she was the only one who dared to make eye contact with me.

I let a few seconds tick by before I said, "Come on, don't be shy. I don't bite."

This garnered a few chuckles.

"I know we have a Facebook page," said Brenda, "but I don't know if it's helping or if we're using it, really."

I nodded.

"Twitter." Claire resituated in her seat. Her soft voice and hypnotic eyes made me forget for a moment that I was in a meeting. She must have noticed, since she cleared her throat to pull me back into the game.

I looked to the senior editor to gauge his mood. He sat glumly in his chair, staring at the tabletop. It didn't take a genius to figure out he was not on board when it came to social media. George, the head of local news, looked to Darrell, and I wondered if he was determining whether or not he should jump into the fray or leave it alone. He must have decided it was best not to poke the bear since he started doodling on his notepad. This wasn't good. I didn't want people to turn to Darrell.

"Darrell, tell me, what do you know about Twitter?" I put him on the spot.

"Twitter," scoffed Darrell. "Is that your plan? Twitter?" He crossed his arms defiantly, showing how often he worked out. His forearms bulged like Popeye's, with all the salt and pepper hairs standing at attention. I would love to hire a cartoonist to draw him, and then I could have Avery post the photo in all the bathroom stalls.

"You didn't answer my question. What do you know about Twitter?" I sat on the edge of the conference table by his side and stared down at the man.

Darrell waved a hand dismissively. "It's a flash in the pan. Don't waste your time, or ours."

"Is just Twitter a flash in the pan? Or all social media?"

"All." He let out an angry snort.

I suspected that would be his answer, and it showed me just how out of touch he was. It was hard to imagine social media ending abruptly. Platforms would change, but as a whole, it was here to stay. "Okay, but just for fun, tell me what you know about Twitter." I waved my hand to get him to share.

"Like I said, this is a waste of time. We should be talking about the paper, not Twitter."

"You're wasting my time, Darrell. Just admit you don't know anything."

Several people gasped. No one, I assumed, spoke to Darrell that way.

Twitter wasn't new. Many social media savvy companies had jumped on the bandwagon years before. This paper wasn't one of those companies, and it was showing.

Darrell sucked in air, obviously irked by my tone. "Don't tell me what I know and don't know, *boss*."

More people gasped.

"Most people call me JJ, Darrell, but you can call me Ms. Cavendish." I winked at him in a commanding way.

Darrell smiled malevolently, but a flicker of fear showed in his countenance. I knew I had to push him further. "If you're an expert, don't be bashful. Tell me about Twitter. How are we using it compared to other media companies?"

He stared at me, flabbergasted.

I continued, "Such as, how often our competition is tweeting? Are they including links? Hashtags? Is it working for them? Are they able to gain subscribers and advertising?"

Darrell reddened.

"That's what I thought. Last year, Twitter was one of the most visited websites." I walked to the whiteboard and grabbed a marker.

"We do have a Twitter account, just in case you don't know," said Darrell.

I froze and locked eyes on the editor. No one in the room moved a muscle. I clicked the cap back onto the marker. "Yes, I know." I motioned to Avery to start the presentation. The paper's Twitter page was displayed. "Looks like we have thousands of followers. That's not bad, but it could be better."

"We have more actual subscribers," countered Darrell.

He meant customers who wanted the paper delivered to their front door.

"Excellent, Darrell. I'm glad we're on the same page. We need to jazz up our Tweets to pull in more followers online. In six months, I want to quadruple our Twitter followers. Not just here in Colorado, but from all over. Coloradoans who have moved away still want to stay connected to their home state. I want to be a part of that connection. To become a part of their social media family."

"Twitter followers. JJ, you need to focus on subscribers. Not Twitter. This is madness." Darrell threw his mechanical pencil down on the blank page of his notebook. I suspected he never planned on jotting anything down, but carried it out of habit.

"Please, call me Ms. Cavendish." I gave him a look of disgust. After I counted to ten in my head, I added, "Paper subscriptions are falling every month, and there's nothing we can do about it. Paper will be dead soon. There's no way around it." I looked Darrell in the eye and then locked eyes briefly with everyone else. "But the company won't be. We have to be innovative. We have to adapt. If we don't, we'll be closing the doors here and everyone will be out of a job, myself included."

This was a lie. If the doors closed on this branch, I would have to tuck my tail between my legs, but I would be heading back to New York. However, I hated failing and had no intention of admitting defeat without doing absolutely everything in my power. And then some.

"What if Twitter is a fad and you've put all your faith in it?" sneered Darrell. "Are we going to pursue Tinder as well?" He cocked his head in triumph.

I was shocked he knew about the online dating service that was used mostly as a way to hook up for sex. "Oh, I didn't know you were more familiar with Tinder. Care to fill the rest of us in about *that*? Any good hookups, I mean *stories* to share?"

Darrell turned three shades of red. Not out of embarrassment, but fury. "I would never use such a filthy app."

"But you know about it." I thought about winking again, but thought better of it. I didn't need any run-ins with the HR department. "In all seriousness, though, I'm not putting all my faith in Twitter. Social media fads come and go. There's no doubt about that. Everyone here probably remembers a company named Myspace. I won't be putting all our eggs in one basket, as you say, Darrell. This is just the first step in a new direction. We have to buff up our presence on the web. We have to think outside the box. Make it sexier, easier to navigate, and more fun. Not just focus on paper.

"Last night, I researched the top companies who used Twitter effectively. We weren't on that list. I don't just mean our paper, but Beale Media as a whole. We need to compete. Even H&R Block was on the list." I let that sink in. "Come on, we're newspaper folks. We're more exciting than tax people, aren't we?

"We can't keep thinking the same as when this paper first opened its doors. Times have changed. The news has changed. Media has changed. Our customers have changed."

I walked around the table as I spoke and noticed Claire tapping her red pen on her notepad. I glanced at it. *You're scaring them. Tone it down.*

Placing a hand on Claire's shoulder briefly, I continued. "That doesn't mean we have to change our core principle. We'll still deliver the news, and we'll still do it the Colorado way. But I want people to notice us and to talk about us. I know I said paper is dead and that may be a terrifying thought for you." I paused. "I'm not trying to scare anyone. I'm being realistic. This is an exciting time. We get to reinvent this company and still hold true to what has made this business a part of the community for the past seventy-five years."

"And who'll be in charge of this Twitter campaign? I have my hands full with the news." Darrell's body language was declaring war.

"I've assigned a team, with Claire and Avery in charge. By the end of the week, I want them to decide who our official tweeter should be. People on our news staff can keep their Twitter accounts, but I do want someone to be our go-to person for the paper's account."

There was murmuring. Claire did her best to prevent her jaw from hitting the floor. I hadn't informed her about this new responsibility.

Hopefully my message was clear. Darrell would not be in charge of any of the new changes at the paper. He would be following orders from now on, not dictating them.

"Claire—she's in advertising!" shouted Darrell.

"Exactly! And it's advertising that's keeping this paper afloat." I refused to back down and let Darrell intimidate me. "We'll have some members from your staff on the team, but Claire and Avery will be in charge."

Darrell looked at his watch. "I have to go." He stood and scooped up his pencil and pad in one vicious swipe.

"Just a second, Darrell. Let's have a quick word outside." I motioned for him to step into the hall. Intentionally, I didn't completely close the door. "Do you have any time later today to have a meeting? Just the two of us?"

"Today?" Darrell scratched his chin arrogantly. "Nope. My son has a recital at school." He started to push by me.

I blocked his way. At first I was going to insist that Darrell miss the recital. But then I remembered most of the people on staff had children, and that wouldn't set the right tone. And didn't Claire mention that her son had a recital today as well? I couldn't have one rule in place for Claire and another for the rest of the staff.

"Tomorrow, then. What time can you meet?" I smiled sweetly even though my tone said it wasn't a request.

"Can't. Meetings all day." Darrell smiled confidently.

"No worries, I arrive early each day. What time do you arrive?"

"Eight, but like I said, I have meetings all day." Again he started to move down the hallway.

"Fine, let's meet at seven," I called after him.

Darrell whipped around to stare me down. "Seven? I'm here till eight most evenings." Darrell's shrill tone made it clear I had struck a nerve. All I needed to do was to give him one more shove.

"I can clear up your evenings and your days, if you'd like." I crossed my arms, showing him that I wasn't going to back down.

"You can't." He stumbled back. "I've been here for thirty years." His voice no longer indicated he was confident in his position.

"Try me, Darrell. Try me." With that I left him sputtering in the hallway and rejoined the group in the conference room. I didn't have to look around to see that everyone had overheard the conversation. The buzz in the room was clear enough. That was even better than the cartoons in the bathroom stalls would have been. Not that the cartoon option was off the table.

"Now where were we?" I asked.

Every single person plastered a fake smile on their faces. Except for Claire. And they started to put ideas on the table. Most were terrible, but they were trying. That was all I wanted. For them to start thinking of new ideas. Get Darrell's way out of their head. Rome wasn't built in a day. Claire stayed mute for most of it and that worried me.

At the end of the meeting, everyone was laughing and enjoying the pizza I'd ordered. The whole Darrell debacle was yesterday's news.

"Thanks, everyone. Let's meet again next week and see where we are. And remember to share any ideas you have with Claire and Avery." I motioned to both women.

People started to filter out of the conference room. Only Avery and Claire remained. Avery was too busy reading her Blackberry to notice that Claire wanted to speak to me in private.

"Avery would you mind getting some files for me?" I asked.

Avery looked up and saw right away why I made the request. "Yes, of course." My assistant left without asking which files I needed. I liked that about her.

Claire sucked in some air and let it out slowly. "You have no idea what you accomplished today."

I knew Claire was referring to Darrell, and I wasn't in the least bit intimidated by the editor. But Claire was agitated, and I wanted to find out why.

"Do you like your new role?" I leaned against the table.

"I'm not talking about that."

"I am. Do you?"

Claire ran a hand through her reddish-brown hair, her tell that she was flustered. "Well, yes, I think it'll be exciting, but do you have any idea what you've done?" Her eyes grew large.

I felt my determination ooze onto the floor. What was bothering her? "What I had to do. I don't enjoy playing the bitch, but let's just say that was part of the game plan corporate put together before I arrived."

Claire stepped back and then nodded curtly. "I see. So there will be layoffs, even though all the talk has been that there won't be."

"Not if I can help it. Some people here don't want to change, but we have to."

"You don't know the full story." Claire's voice bordered on pleading.

"I'm all ears. Please tell me." I patted the table next to me.

Claire looked around nervously. "Not here. I'll text you on your cell."

My cell. My private cell. The news didn't have to do with the company, but with Claire. I was intrigued and hesitant. How was she connected to Darrell? Most here didn't like the man. I hadn't seen them working together. My gut told me I was missing the obvious, but my brain was clueless.

"Sounds good." I kept my voice steady and positive, just in case others were listening. "I have some books for you and your new team to read. Avery will bring them down for you. Please let me know what else you need." I placed a hand on Claire's shoulder and stroked her neck with a finger. I could see some of her tension melt. "All of us are in this together." I let my hand linger for a moment, before retreating to the staircase.

Ten minutes later, I received a text from Claire asking me to come by her house that night around eight. Very intriguing.

I PARKED MY car on the street in front of Claire's house. My bravado was disappearing faster than a piece of thin tissue paper in the rain. Earlier I had convinced myself that I could handle seeing Claire in her home with her son, Ian. But how would I handle seeing her in a life that didn't include me? It wasn't like I hadn't gone on with my life after that night. So had Claire, of course. She was the director of advertising. Had a son. A nice house. Could I fit into her life?

Claire stepped out front and waved, looking happy and completely relaxed. I wish I could've said the same.

I pretended I was on the phone and not terrified of coming inside. I motioned just a minute and jabbered into my Blackberry, not speaking to anyone.

Smooth, JJ. Real smooth.

The time for stalling was over, and I got out of my car and tentatively approached Claire. I felt like I was in a slow-motion movie scene right before someone approached a coffin in the funeral parlor to discover their own body in the casket.

Claire waited patiently until I was in arm's length. She pulled me to her and kissed my cheek, followed by an affectionate squeeze. A lover's squeeze, not a best friend one.

Inside I was freaking out. "Hello." My tone was businesslike.

Claire swatted my arm. "Work's over, JJ. Loosen up." Then she took my hand and led me into her home. Claire continued to clutch my hand and didn't let go until we were in the kitchen. Then she kissed me passionately.

I shuffled back, shocked. "Uh, where's Ian?"

Claire laughed. "Relax. Ian's in his room, playing a video game. What's wrong with you?" Claire turned and grabbed a bottle of wine. "Would you mind opening this while I finish preparing dinner?"

Claire opened the oven and pulled out a lasagna, which obviously was store-bought.

"I see you still don't cook," I teased as I inserted the corkscrew. Deftly, I uncorked the wine and poured a glass for Claire. I hoped she would get the hint and not ask why I wasn't having a glass.

"Earth to JJ. The wine is for both of us." Claire pushed a glass toward me. "I cook occasionally, but not usually on work nights. Who has the time?" She shrugged and motioned to the empty wineglass again.

"That's okay. I'm not much of a wine drinker." Immediately the color rushed to my face, tattling on me that I was lying.

"Since when?" Her puzzled face showed concern.

"Uh …" I rubbed the back of my neck, which was tightening, and I wondered if I looked like someone who would rather jump off a hundred-foot cliff than answer the question.

Realization spread across Claire's face. "Does it have something to do with your tattoo?"

"You can say that."

"Well, what would you like? I have Coke, Dr. Pepper, and sparkling water." Claire's demeanor indicated she wasn't going to push me on the issue. Not right now at least.

"Sparkling water would be great."

Claire pulled a plastic green bottle out of the fridge and poured it into my empty wineglass. "Grab your drink and plate. Let's eat in the dining room. Might as well use it at least once this year." She winked at me. All the tension she'd displayed after the meeting was gone.

The room was dark and clearly unused. Claire had set the table in anticipation of tonight's meal but didn't have enough time to make it look lived in.

"Is it just the two of us?" I asked.

"Yeah, Ian ate earlier. He's on a fish sticks and mac and cheese kick at the moment. And while this"—she motioned to the lasagna—"doesn't count as gourmet, I couldn't subject you to fish sticks."

We ate in silence. Claire sipped her wine and studied me. "Can I ask you something?"

Here we go. The alcohol question, I thought. "Sure." I accidentally turned it into a three-syllable word.

"Why are you so nervous tonight?" She tapped her fingernails against the wineglass.

It wasn't the question I'd expected. "It's just weird. Being here in *your* home."

"Why?"

"I don't know. It just is."

"Are you afraid of meeting Ian?"

"What? No, of course not. I would love to meet your son."

"Then what is it? Because this weekend, you weren't this weird. And earlier today you strutted around in that meeting like you owned the place. What's wrong?"

I placed a hand on Claire's. "Nothing. Nothing's wrong."

"Are you afraid I'm going to yell at you?" She wouldn't let it go.

"No, why? Are you?" I smiled, starting to feel more like myself.

"Maybe."

"Shall we get to it then? The yelling?" I motioned to Claire to say what she wanted to say.

She paused. "Why did you have to humiliate Darrell like that? In front of all of us?"

"I didn't want to. That wasn't my intention this morning when I started the meeting." Okay, this wasn't entirely true, but I felt it was best to stay mute on my over-reaching goal.

"You could have handled it differently. And then threatening his job. Really?" She quirked an eyebrow out of disgust.

"There are always sacrificial lambs when a new boss comes to town." The explanation sounded lame even to me, and she was smart enough to sense there was more to it. Looking back, I realized that maybe I should have handled it better.

"So if it was me who challenged you this morning, would you have acted the same way?"

"What? Of course not. Besides, you wouldn't do that."

"Why? Because I'm not brave enough?" Her voice sizzled with irritation.

I set my fork down. "That's not what I said. You don't resist change. You brought up Twitter this weekend, in fact. Darrell had to be put in his place. He caused major problems for the previous corporate guy, and I had been warned to reel him in and quick. Not everything I do is my idea. I have bosses who know everything I do. Do you think Avery is just my assistant?"

"Are you suggesting Avery is a spy for corporate?" Claire laughed, and then stopped when she saw I wasn't kidding.

"Maybe yes. Maybe no. But corporate has eyes and ears everywhere."

"And what's your proof?" I could tell by her eyes she wasn't buying it.

"Because I was once an Avery," I confessed, feeling smaller than an ant.

Claire pushed her chair back from the table. She hadn't touched much of her meal. "Is that how you advanced so quickly? You were a mole?"

"It wasn't the only reason. But I proved early on I could be trusted and that I could toe the party line. Business is business, Claire. It's hardly ever pretty."

"And that's that. No gray areas."

"I wouldn't say that. Why are you fixated on this? Darrell is a shitty editor. He's driven the news department into the ground. It's not just corporate that thinks that. Many of your peers have pleaded with us to get rid of him."

"I don't want him to go."

"The decision isn't yours to make." My voice was firm.

"And what if I say don't do it?"

"You aren't my boss." I stared at her without blinking.

"So I don't have a say in anything that happens at the paper? Is that what you're telling me?" She threw her napkin on top of her plate.

"You have a say in what happens in your department. You are not on the news floor." It was hard to control my annoyance. Why was she fighting me on this?

"And you have a say over everything. The rest of us peons should just toe the line."

I sighed heavily. "What's this really about? Me? My management style? I have to act tough. Do you know what it's like being a female in charge?"

"Do I know what it's like?" She plunked her wineglass. "I run the advertising department. Most of the sales reps are men. Of course I get it."

"Then why are you fighting me on this? What's Darrell to you?"

"He's Ian's father," she blurted out and then rushed out of the room.

I sat at the table, thunderstruck. Ian's father. Were Darrell and Claire lovers? Married? Divorced?

Getting up from the table, I walked through the home, searching for her. Stumbling over some Legos in the family room, I bumped into a bookshelf and saw photos of Claire. Of Ian. Claire's parents. Claire and Ian together. But there were no photos of men, except Claire's father. No Darrell.

A flash on the back deck caught my attention. I opened the door and found Claire sitting on a wicker couch, smoking angrily.

I reached for Claire's cigarettes and lit one. "I think I'm missing something," I said after exhaling.

"Just one thing?" Claire hissed.

"Are you and Darrell a couple?"

Claire took a drag on her cigarette. "Nope." Smoke swirled out of her nostrils.

"So you and Darrell?" I wasn't sure how to proceed with caution. Did they have an office fling? A serious relationship? It was hard to phrase a question without letting my feelings be known. Darrell was the last person I would have thought Claire would be with. Not only was he stodgy, but he was ten years older, albeit he did take great care of himself. For an older man, he could be considered a catch if he got rid of his ridiculous glasses and bad attitude.

"We used to be friends. Have drinks. Talk. Commiserate. Darrell was going through a difficult divorce. I had recently ended yet another pointless relationship. We got drunk one night, hooked up, and ..."

"And Ian." I filled in the blank.

"And Ian. Darrell wanted to marry me. Make an honest woman of me, but I didn't love him like that." Claire stubbed out her cigarette and lit another. "I couldn't do that to Darrell. And not to Ian. My son is my whole world."

I nodded, finally understanding.

"I know you think Darrell is an ass." She put a hand up to silence me. "Everyone does these days. But you didn't know him back then. Before his divorce he was quite charming, funny, and sweet. His ex-wife did a number on him. He was madly in love with her, but she had an affair and turned his kids against him, filling their heads with lies. They still don't talk to him.

"Darrell makes child support payments. Spends some weeknights and every other weekend with Ian. Never misses any of his recitals or other things most men in his position would be too busy for. Hell, he even attended Lamaze classes with me. He's a good father. You may not respect him at work, but he's a good man. A decent, kind man who adores Ian. Given the situation, I couldn't have hoped for a better father for my son."

I stared hard into the darkness behind her house, wishing I could disappear in the void.

"Okay."

"Okay, what?" Claire didn't try to hide her frustration.

"Okay. I get it. Can you help me find a way to get through to Darrell? He can't try to humiliate me in meetings and act like he's still in charge."

"He has been in charge. For years he ran the paper. We didn't have bigwigs from corporate bossing us around." She was defending him, but I sensed from her body language she wasn't his biggest fan at work. Claire was both a realist and an idealist.

"I know, and I recognize that this is hard for him. But he has to let me do my job." I turned to face Claire. "If I don't, it won't just be Darrell out of a job."

I saw the fear in Claire's expression and sat down next to her.

Claire rested her head on my shoulder. "Please. No one at the paper knows about Darrell being Ian's father."

"I would never say a thing."

"Not even to Darrell."

I put my pinky finger out. It was our thing: the pinky swear. It was the most sacred of vows we made to each other back in the day. She hooked her pinky with mine. I felt comforted and filled with dread. My mind was reeling with ways to make this work. First thing in the morning, I was contacting a headhunter. Not for me, but for Darrell.

I SPENT THE night at Claire's. Closing my eyes, I remembered our evening together after talking on the deck. We took Ian for ice cream, and I was floored by how much he looked like Darrell. But Ian didn't have his father's chip on his shoulder. He was a sweet boy who loved his mom.

I wondered if Claire was upset when she woke to find me gone. Around four, the trash truck rattled through the neighborhood making one hell of a racket. Claire didn't stir, probably used to the noise. I slipped out, not wanting to startle Ian in the morning. The last thing I needed was for Ian to ask his father why I was staying the night at his mom's house.

I sat in my office, mentally preparing for the meeting with Darrell. My therapist trained me to imagine my happy place when tense. I sat at my desk, with my eyes closed, imagining I was sitting on the beach, listening to the waves.

A rustling outside my office door drew my attention, and Darrell swaggered in at 7:01. He sat down without being asked.

"Morning." His tone was gruff.

"Good morning, Darrell. How was your son's recital?"

"Fine." He clearly didn't want to talk about his son.

I wasn't comfortable with the subject, either. I was still in shock about the bomb Claire had dropped last night and had no clue how to handle the fallout.

"Before you start, I spoke with Bill last night."

I perked up in my chair. "Oh." I had spoken with Bill as well before heading to Claire's.

"Yeah, so I'm not thrilled with the idea, but count me in." His eyes bounced all over the room, but never landed on me. The expression on his face was not the expression of a man who supported any ideas that weren't his own. It was a look of defiant defeat.

"Good to hear."

Darrell cleared his throat, and the sound made me gag. *Claire slept with this man?*

"Anything else, *boss*?" He looked me in the eyes.

I wanted to put the man in his place, again. "Nope. Not unless there's something you want to say."

"Can't think of anything."

We stared at each other. Finally, Darrell stood. "Well, I have work to do."

I nodded, dismissing him.

As soon as the door was closed, I let out a long breath and whispered, "What an ass."

Only Claire could get me into this dilemma. I rubbed my head, frustrated. Every job had a challenge. Managing Darrell might be my biggest yet.

At forty-four, I realized I had never been with a woman who had a child. Usually that was a deal breaker. Now the idea appealed to me. I was getting soft.

Now I was dealing with a woman who had a child with an asshole father that I had to see every day and who I had to rein in to convince corporate that we didn't need to fire him. It would probably be easier to get a Buddhist to intentionally step on an ant, and I imagined that would be nearly impossible.

My desk phone rang.

"JJ Cavendish."

"Hello, JJ Cavendish. No coffee this morning." Claire's flirty voice made the last fifteen minutes worth it.

"Tell me what kind you want and I'll bring it to you."

"Yes!" I imagined her high-fiving herself. Claire rattled off her order, and I left the office immediately, not embarrassed at all by my lovesick puppy attitude. It felt good to be this giddy. I felt alive.

I returned with Claire's coffee, a skinny macchiato, and several large containers of coffee for the morning staff along with dozens of donuts. I bumped into Tim, the creepy salesman, in the parking lot and enlisted his help to carry it all in. I had called Avery a few minutes earlier, and she was already heading to my car.

"Is this for us?" asked Tim, when he saw the loot in the back seat.

"Yep."

"Do we get this every day?"

I laughed. "Nope, but I was feeling nice this morning."

Tim flashed an overly friendly smile that bordered on seductive. "I like you already." He brushed against my shoulder.

I dashed for the door, seeking refuge among others, and left Kung Fu Avery to fend for herself. Something told me she wouldn't have any issues putting Tim, or any other man, in his place. I imagined her karate chopping Tim without wrinkling her suit. Besides, even though we never discussed it, I was certain she played on my team. When we still lived in New York, occasionally I would bump into her at a gay event. She never went out of her way to let everyone know she was a lesbian, but she never went out of her way to hide it either. I liked that about her. Avery was confident, hard-to-pin-down, and mentally tough. She would make a great executive one day.

Claire couldn't help chuckling when she saw all the employees flocking to the coffee and donuts. "They're like kids in a candy store."

Brenda said, "I better grab one before they're gone. You want your fave, Claire? Chocolate with sprinkles?"

Claire nodded.

I beamed. This trick worked wherever I went. One minute they feared you. The next, after giving them a donut, they loved you.

Brenda handed Claire her donut before retreating to her office.

"You ready for our meeting?" I motioned for Claire to follow me upstairs.

We bumped into Darrell on the stairs.

"Good morning, Darrell," said Claire in a singsong voice.

Darrell bit into a bear claw and grunted.

I left my office door open for Avery and the rest of the team to join us after they grabbed coffee and donuts. While we were still alone I whispered, "He's so charming."

Claire shook her head threateningly.

"Now. Twitter. Tell me what you know, what you need to know, and how I can help." I flipped on my boss façade, and we launched into a strategy meeting. The others in the group straggled in with their booty, eager to impress probably in hopes I'd keep bringing in free food and drinks. That motivated them more than the fear that the paper would close.

chapter seven

One Saturday night, Claire and I were soaking in a hot tub in her backyard. Claire held a glass of red wine in her hand and inspected it like it was an offensive weed in a prize-winning garden.

"Does it bother you?" she asked.

"What?" It was a cold March night, and I had just popped up from immersing myself completely in the hot water to take the chill out of my bones. I wiped droplets out of my eyes.

"That I'm having a glass of wine. That every evening we're together, which has been often when Ian is with his dad …" Claire raised her eyebrows seductively. "I still have a glass of wine and … you don't."

"No. I was never much of a wine drinker—too vinegary for me. I only drank it in school if it was the only option."

"That's not what I mean and you know that." Claire splashed water at me.

"I know. It's not something I like to talk about, though." I observed the moon and all the stars. In New York, I'd hardly seen the sky, let alone stars.

"Hey, that's not fair. I told you my big secret."

"What? That you eat a bag of M&Ms at your desk before most of your staff reports for the day," I teased.

"Don't start with me. You are the only person besides my parents who I've told that Darrell is Ian's father."

"What name is on the birth certificate?"

"I didn't list Darrell." Claire let out an exasperated growl. "And you're doing that thing you always do."

"What's that?" Claire floated over and wrapped her arms around me, maybe in hopes to squeeze the stubbornness out. "Deflect. You're a pro at not answering personal questions, but you know how to fish for the information you want. Please, tell me."

"You know how everyone calls me the Miracle Girl?" She nodded. "Have you heard the reason why they call me that at work?"

"I've heard a few theories. One: your meteoric rise. Two: your awesome adventures and how you escape animal attacks, like a bear ravaging your tent." She winked. "Three: you are a superhero." Claire's smile warmed my heart.

"I've heard those as well and a few others. All are wrong. Only one person knows the true reason for the name, and she's the one who gave me the nickname."

"Who?"

"Cora Matthews."

Claire whistled. "The CEO."

"Yeah, Cora became my mentor early on in my career, long before she became the top dog."

My body stiffened, and Claire let her arms fall away from me, knowing I needed space to tell the story.

"Cora knew I had a problem." I turned to face Claire. "It wasn't just booze. I spent most of my days chasing the dragon."

Claire tilted her head, confused. "Chasing the dragon … are you referring to pot?"

I stifled a laugh. "No. I'm not referring to Puff the Magic Dragon. I was into blow, snow, candy cane, white girl, wacky dust … There are many words for it, but you're probably more familiar with the name cocaine."

Claire let out a gasp and put her hand to her chest. Even in school, Claire never did any hard drugs and only smoked weed a couple of times, both times with me, the bad influence.

"I won't lie; I was hooked. Cora guessed I had a problem, and she tried getting me to go straight. I kept telling her I was fine. I could handle it.

And for the most part I *was* handling it. I never missed a day of work. I was excelling at work—advancing even. I had everything under control." I skimmed my hand along the water.

I took a deep breath, preparing for the big confession.

"Then everything was out of control. I don't even know how or why. One day, I was managing it all. The next, I was screwing up at work, when I bothered to go. Most of the time I said I was working in the field—that meant I was too amped up to come in. Or too sick.

"When Cora hadn't heard from me in a couple of days, she came to my apartment and found me."

"What do you mean *found* you?" Claire's voice was concerned.

"I was a complete mess and damn lucky I hadn't overdosed."

"Oh, JJ."

I nodded, unable to speak yet.

"What happened?"

"Cora gave me an ultimatum: go to rehab or lose my job. If I chose option A, she'd keep my addiction quiet. Save my career in addition to my life. If I went with option B, she'd fire me publically and state the reason, which would have ruined me."

Claire sucked in some air indignantly.

"I can't blame her. She trusted me, and her reputation was on the line. Not just mine."

"What'd you choose?"

"I went to rehab, of course." I shrugged.

Claire's face clearly showed relief, even in the faint light of the moon.

"And then I started using as soon as I got out."

Claire shook her head, looking like she was unable to say how she felt without showing her disappointment. I had seen that look on many faces, but seeing it on hers was the worst.

"Cora figured it out. She didn't give me an ultimatum this time, though. I tried rehab again, after getting arrested for drunk driving, to no avail. Cora was patient. She knew sooner or later I would hit rock bottom, and it didn't take long. I called her one morning." My voice broke, and I looked up to the moon with glistening eyes, wishing I was there instead of in the hot tub baring my soul.

Claire patiently waited, not wanting to push.

"I woke up one morning … and I was in rough shape." I didn't want to say what happened, but I had to say it. Needed to say it. And saying it to Claire—well, she should know. "It was a Sunday. Not that I knew that when I was on the phone. I went out Friday night, and that was the last thing I remembered. When I woke up that Sunday, I was bruised and bloodied. And that's not all. I don't know if I was a willing participant since I have no memory, but I was sore … you know down there." I motioned to my crotch.

Claire bit her quivering lower lip, doing her best to stay calm.

"Cora took me to the hospital once she found me. I didn't even know where I was when I called her. Some random motel and no one was in sight. The motel room was filthy—well, you can probably fill in the blanks. I'm sure you've seen enough episodes of *Law and Order: SVU* to envision such a fleabag room." I tried to laugh it off, but couldn't. Too many images flooded my brain. I blinked excessively before continuing.

"They did a rape kit—" My voice stumbled over the word rape. "But … there wasn't enough evidence, and I didn't have any recollection—I was more concerned about keeping everything quiet. Cora miraculously kept my name out of the press, and the cops didn't follow up much since Cora told them I didn't want them to because it wasn't clear what really happened that night. They knew from the tests that I was fucking out of my mind. Completely blotto on coke and booze."

Claire reached out to touch me and then pulled her hand back, unsure. "I'm sorry—"

"It's okay." I rubbed my face. "When I was released from the hospital I got on a plane and entered rehab for the third time. Cora flew with me and checked me in. To this day she has never told a soul. But when I came back, she said offhandedly in a meeting that her miracle girl was back. People liked the nickname, even though they didn't know what it really meant. Only Cora and I knew. A mystique developed around the moniker, and every time I hear it, I cringe. Waking up in that motel—it was the worst day of my life. Cora rues the day she first used that nickname, but what can she do. She's a media woman and such name recognition from my nickname helps in the biz. Even I use it to my advantage." I shrugged, and the action made me feel vulnerable.

"When did all this happen?"

"Ten years ago. I've been clean ten years."

"No relapses … not after ...?" Claire's unfinished sentence hung in the air.

"One minor blip."

"Do you miss it?"

I cocked an eyebrow. "Coke?" Claire nodded. "I miss the anticipation of it."

She nodded again, even though I knew she had no idea what that meant. No one did unless they tried it. Even sitting here with her, I wanted that jolt.

"Do you ever feel like … you know, just trying it?"

"All the time. Like this morning. I saw an Ann Taylor button bag—"

"A button bag?" Claire butted in, laughing, and then looked away guilty.

"My dealer sometimes sold me coke that he placed in button bags. Every time I see one of those bags I get this craving."

"But you don't … risk it," she whispered.

I shook my head. "I don't even take cough medicine." I patted my back, indicating my tattoo. "I got this tattoo after five years of kicking the habit. Cora was there for one of the sessions. It helps remind me of what I've overcome and how close I was to losing everything."

"And the 'remember' tattoo?"

"To remind me that I'm not the Miracle Girl. Not the way people think."

We were silent for a while, until Claire broke it. "Were you and Cora an item?"

I knew my face showed my surprise. No one had ever guessed about that. "Uh, we did have a relationship—but no one can know about that." I sat up straight. "She's married now. Has a kid."

Claire put her hand on my shoulder. "Don't worry. I won't tell a soul about any of it."

"How did you guess? About Cora, I mean?"

She raised her left shoulder like she was scratching her ear. "From what I've heard, she isn't the most patient person in the world, but she was with you—for you to get your act together. There had to be a reason besides business."

"You read people well. Maybe I should promote you to be my number two." I wasn't joking.

"Aw, how romantic. Every girl dreams of being called her lover's number two."

I laughed. "You see! The business person in me missed that. You could really help me with the personal aspects. I'm good with spreadsheets, reports, and all that jazz."

Claire rested her head against the tub. "I'm perfectly happy in my role, and I'm not sure I want to be that woman. The one who sleeps with the boss and then gets a promotion. And if people find out about Darrell and then you—my reputation will be shot. Not even the small paper in Fort Collins that's been trying to recruit me will want me. Besides, you have a great assistant. Trust Avery more."

"What paper is recruiting you?" My voice was alarmed.

"*Fort Collins Gazette*. I've turned them down twice now. I want Ian to be close to his father."

I sighed my relief about the paper. The seconds ticked by with neither of us speaking and made me uncomfortable. Claire was the first woman I had told everything to about my stints in rehab, and I worried it would change things between us.

"Can you do me a favor? Try not to treat me with kid gloves. If you want a glass of wine, have it. And I know the other news might affect things. It was a long time ago. I'm not saying it doesn't affect me; it does. I just don't want to ruin … what we have. Especially now that I have you back in my life."

She smiled.

"God I've missed you." She touched my cheek gently. "My Claire," I whispered before resting my head on her shoulder.

chapter eight

"Blogs!" hollered Darrell. "You want us to hire bloggers? We're a newspaper, not WordPress."

I sat on the edge of the far table in the conference room, and eased off one of my four-inch heels. I regretted the decision to wear them. I had a meeting later with the governor and needed to look more glamorous than usual. My black pencil skirt hitched up a bit, and Claire smiled. Adjusting my skirt and silk lavender blouse, I tried my best to maintain my cool and intimidate the officious editor. At the other end of the long table, Darrel adjusted his hideous black-framed glasses. With my arms crossed I answered, "Yes, that's exactly what I mean."

"First it was Twitter. Now blogs. Make up your fucking mind." Darrell waved an arm in the air.

Ten pairs of eyes stared at us like they were watching tennis, back and forth, and they were dying to see how I would handle his last potshot. I chose to ignore his f-bomb. That type of language was the norm in the newspaper business. "I haven't given up on Twitter. And have you ever heard of *The Huffington Post*? Or the *Drudge Report*, Darrell?"

Darrell, shell-shocked, shook his head exasperated. "They publish garbage."

"Really?" I sat farther back on the table. "*The Huffington Post* has won a Pulitzer, and the *Drudge Report* was the first to break the Monica Lewinsky story."

"I don't think we should lower our standards just because the average citizen craves junk news."

"Oh, Darrell, I don't even know where to start with that statement." I smiled, knowing I had the upper hand. "Who are we to judge what type of news to report on? What you might consider junk news is what thousands of others crave. But let's look at this from a different angle. A former media advisor to Bush Jr. has admitted that he used to check the *Drudge Report* around thirty times a day. Tell me, do you think any media advisors to Obama are checking our paper or website for stories every day or ever for that matter?"

"But it's muckraking," he defended.

A small smile crept onto Claire's face. She was the only one in the room who knew my fascination and admiration of the famous muckrakers from the early 1900s. Ida Tarbell, Lincoln Steffens, and Ray Baker were the most famous. Darrell's insult was actually a compliment. And he'd used the wrong term. He meant to say it was yellow journalism, which was pure sensationalism and not based on facts. Back in the day, muckrakers delved deep for all the facts.

I decided not to give Darrell a history lesson. "Exactly! Sites like *Drudge*, *Huffington*, and even *TMZ* receive millions of hits a day. A day!" I slammed my hand down on the table.

"*TMZ*! Are you going to expect our photographers to chase celebrities now? Stalk Peyton Manning. Track down Amy Adams when she visits?" Darrell turned to the staff, victorious. "Come on, help me name other famous people affiliated with Colorado."

"Tim Allen."

"David Fincher."

"Jessica Biel lived in Boulder."

"Don Cheadle attended East High School in Denver."

"Lon Chaney."

Everyone looked to Claire.

"What? He was born in Colorado Springs." Her voice was steady, but a hint of crimson tinted her cheeks.

"The silent actor has been dead for eighty-something years," said Darrell in a supercilious tone.

I came to Claire's defense. "If one of our photographers can get a photo of his ghost, I'm on board. I can see the headline now, 'The Ghost with a Thousand Faces.'" I paused to direct my attention back to Darrell. "And I know you are trying to convince me that we're heading down the wrong path, but all you're doing is convincing me that we are on the right path. The fact that several of you can spout off names of famous Coloradoans proves that even stuffy newspaper people know about them. What did you call it Darrell, junk news? Actually, I think we should have a blog titled Junk News."

Several people around the table smiled, and the rest nodded their heads approvingly. Only Darrell refused to budge one iota.

"Let me ask you one thing, JJ."

I nodded my agreement.

"If we got the scoop on your dirty laundry, would you give us permission to print it? Think about that, before you go down this road. It's a slippery slope." He tapped the table with his empty notepad.

I sucked in some air. "If your team got the scoop on me, I wouldn't hesitate about going to press. That's our fucking job." I felt sick saying this in front of Claire. She knew about my past, the secret I was desperate to keep out of the news. I couldn't look in her direction. Would I hesitate? Or would I ask Cora to save me again? I hoped I wouldn't have to find out.

He didn't storm from the room this time. But during the remainder of the meeting, Darrell kept his arms crossed, looking defiant and huffing to himself whenever an idea was proposed.

When it came time to hear the update from news, Darrell started to speak about a series his life writers were working on for Easter. Normally in meetings I avoided looking at him for any length of time since I couldn't stand the sight of him, but this morning, I examined the side of his head and noticed something disturbing. There was hair growing on top of his ears. Surely this was a new development. Wouldn't I have noticed his Hobbit ears earlier even if I hardly ever looked at the man?

I held my cell phone eye level and squinted so everyone thought I was checking my e-mail. This wasn't out of the ordinary for me. Instead, I was squinting at Darrell's ear hair. Did he have to shave his ears? Did his barber clip them each time he got a haircut? Darrell's military-style hair probably needed trimming every three weeks. Did his ears?

Then I remembered Claire had had sex with this man. She had fucked a man who had hair sprouting from his ears. Just thinking of this made me want to puke in my mouth.

I felt close to heaving, so I cut Darrell off and started to wrap up the meeting. "Any final ideas before we call it a day?"

Avery raised her hand. No one else at the meeting raised their hand before they spoke, but the young assistant felt like she should. Everyone else in the room was a department head and had proven their salt, mostly. She was the newbie and outsider, and I appreciated the fact that she recognized that. It would make those in the room like her more and hopefully open up to her. I needed intel. Was desperate for it, actually.

"Avery, please, don't be shy." I motioned for her to speak.

"What if we ran a contest for a citizen blogger?"

"A citizen blogger?" I was mulling over the idea, and no one in the room knew how to react. "That's a wonderful idea! And we can leave the vote up to the public. Run the blog entries that are worthwhile and have the readers vote for who they want."

Darrell sucked in so much air I wondered if his nostrils burned from oxygen overload. To his credit, he remained quiet, but his face started to turn purple. I worried the poor man was having a coronary. Would it be wrong to pray that was the case?

"You know we could have more than one citizen blogger. One for sports, local politics, entertainment ..." Claire motioned etcetera with her hand, and Darrell stared at her like she had just set herself on fire.

"I love it. Avery work with Claire's team to roll out the contest. I want it started by next week." With that, I dismissed everyone.

chapter nine

"Why are you here?" Ian's blue eyes looked at me quizzically. I didn't sense any malice in his question, only child-like honesty. Children would make great interviewers if only their attention spans held out.

It had been months since Claire and I settled into our routine of me staying the night when Ian was with his father or grandparents. I rarely stayed over when he was home. The schedule was ideal for both of us. Claire still had her one-on-one time with her son, and I would cram in as much work as possible on my nights away. Claire didn't know how to keep Ian from mentioning me to Darrell, but she wanted me to interact with her son. Her solution was to invite me over for dinner.

"Ian!" Claire's stern voice didn't startle the boy. "Don't be rude to our guest for dinner."

"Are you cooking?" asked the curious boy.

"Yes, of course. Why do you look so surprised?" Claire opened the oven and peeked under the aluminum foil to reveal a massive chunk of meat.

Ian shook his head, but I suspected if I wasn't there, he would have said something snarky. I really wanted to know, but didn't know the boy well enough to push him to reveal.

Claire smiled at her son. "Why don't you go upstairs and play until dinner's ready?"

Ian shot out of the kitchen like a rabbit being chased by a fox.

"My mother says someday he'll be able to carry on a conversation that doesn't involve his Xbox." She smiled and let out a long breath. "He reminds me of his father quite a bit, actually."

"Does Darrell have an Xbox?" I teased. The thought of the pompous editor playing video games tickled me.

"He does actually. He and Ian play every night. A Tolkien-like adventure game of some sort. Why don't you ask Darrell about it tomorrow? I'm sure he would be able to bore you to death." Claire's look challenged me to say something snide about her son's father.

I sipped my water to force down the snotty comment forming in my head. "What's for dinner? It smells delicious."

Her knowing look informed me that she knew I was purposefully changing the subject to safer waters. "Beef tenderloin. I don't cook often, but when I do, I like to make a lot of it to feed us for a week."

We chatted in the kitchen until it was time for dinner. The smells in the kitchen made my mouth water. When she said it was time to eat, I almost did a cartwheel. My house hunting had been put on an indefinite hold. The numbers at the paper weren't looking that great. Cora moved me out of the five-star hotel and into corporate housing near the office. She thought the location was great so I could run to and from work, which I did when I lived in New York after rehab to combat the urge to hop into a bar after work. It was sweet of Cora to think of that, but I also knew this was part of her plan. To cultivate the image of a young, active publisher at the helm. The place was nice, but not homey. I missed having a place of my own. However, the maid service was a perk.

Claire placed Ian's plate in front of him. At first the boy was fidgeting too much to notice anything, but as soon as he glanced down at his food his eyebrows sprang up in alarm. Claire couldn't see her son's reaction from her vantage point. After serving my plate and setting hers down, she took her seat. Ian's agitated state increased by the second, and I sensed a breakdown was on the horizon.

"Bon appétit." Claire smiled and raised her knife and fork to cut into the tenderloin.

"Mom!" Ian shouted. He could barely remain in his seat. How did the boy wiggle so much and not tip over?

"What, honey?" Her tone was motherly and assuring.

He frantically pointed to her plate and then to his. "Don't eat that!"

Claire scrunched her forehead and poked the meat with her fork. "Why not?" she asked.

He leaned across the table and whispered behind his hand, "I think Rocky pooped in the sauce."

Claire burst into a loud guffaw. This agitated Ian further, and his already pink face resembled an overripe cherry ready to pop.

I looked to Ian and then to Claire, completely in the dark. Who was Rocky, and why did he mess with the sauce? And how in the world did Ian know?

"Oh, Ian. Those are peppercorns."

Ian eyed his plate suspiciously as he nudged a peppercorn with his fork. I was surprised to see peppercorns in the sauce and wondered if she'd done it for my benefit. She wasn't a fan of spice.

Claire turned to me. "Rocky is Ian's rabbit. He thinks the peppercorns are rabbit turds." She laughed again, even though she was trying hard to hold it in.

Ian was obviously embarrassed, and his defiant look made me almost burst into laughter. I did my best to force the merriment down by clamping on my lower lip.

Ian continued to stir the peppercorns on his plate. "I don't like them," he muttered through gritted teeth.

"How would you know? You've never had them." Claire smiled breezily before taking a bite of her beef.

"Have to!"

"When? I know your father doesn't cook."

Ian stabbed a roasted potato like he was murdering it. "At school." Then he shoved a massive bite of potato into his tiny mouth and did his best to chew without choking.

"You have a gourmet cafeteria, then. When I was your age, they only served us bread and water." She flashed me a knowing smile.

This rankled Ian further.

"And they made us sit outside to eat, even in a blizzard," I added, trying to ease the tension.

It didn't work. Claire giggled, but Ian shot me a look, informing me to butt out of the situation.

Claire took another bite of the beef and made a show of how much she enjoyed the flavor for Ian's benefit.

Several seconds ticked by.

I had a bite. Claire was never known for her cooking skills in the past, but I was impressed with this meal. I nodded approvingly.

"You like it?" She fished for a compliment.

"I do. These are the most delicious rabbit turds I've ever eaten."

Ian burst into a fit of giggles before he could cover his mouth so he wouldn't betray that he was no longer cranky. He was able to control his facial expression, but failed dimming the sparkle of amusement in his eyes. He had his mother's long lashes and his father's stubbornness.

"Have you eaten a lot of rabbit turds?" Claire asked.

"Yes. At school," I said.

This time Ian laughed and made no attempt to hide his enjoyment. I had won him over, with Claire's assistance. His stony reserve transformed into a genuine smile that only a child could flash. Then he sampled some of the beef. In between chewing he said, "Best rabbit turds ever!" Bits of food dribbled out of his overstuffed mouth, and to my surprise, he dabbed his mouth with his napkin.

THE FOLLOWING MONDAY I was back in the conference room with the team. I really hated starting my work week off this way. Not just because of Darrell, but it was nearly impossible to get the team to focus on the issue at hand. After the first few fruitful meetings, their concentration fell into a black abyss. I was amazed that Henry, the previous corporate guy, was able to stick it out for seven months. I'd been here three and, at times, wanted to wave the white flag and go back home. It was like everyone, but Claire and Avery, were completely oblivious that I was doing my best to save this paper.

"What's that smell?" Brenda's hair was crazier than normal and looked like she had styled it by putting her finger in a light socket. Not once, but several times for volume. Her wrinkled shirt and oversized cardigan along with her wire-framed glasses added to her mad scientist look.

Several in the conference room sniffed loudly.

"I don't know, but it seems familiar," replied Darrell. "Reminds me of college."

Claire looked at me sympathetically. She was the only one who knew about my neck issue, and she'd seen me slather Bengay on it earlier that morning. I had hoped extra perfume would counteract the fumes. Obviously not.

"So, Brenda, where are you on the campaign to increase online circulation?" I tried to refocus everyone's attention back to the matter at hand—saving the paper and their jobs.

She sniffed again in my direction. "It's you." The crazy-haired woman crinkled her nose in disgust. "Is that a perfume they sell back East?" There was a hint of sarcasm hidden in her nasally tone, even though her eyes didn't betray her true feelings. It was hard to see her eyes behind her thick lenses.

"I think they sell it everywhere. Not just back East," I answered, before collapsing back into my seat at the head of the table. Each week the director's meeting deteriorated before we accomplished anything. This one was falling apart much sooner than normal.

Darrell snapped his fingers. "Bengay. That's the smell."

"I hurt my neck. Is that a problem for any of you?" I asked with as much dignity as I could muster. Not even Claire's massage or other activities could fix it this time. I hated knowing it would be several days before I could turn my head to the left again. Claire had taken my car keys away from me earlier that morning and driven me to work since running was out of the question.

"I've always liked the smell of Bengay," announced Claire.

"No you don't," said Darrell. "No one likes that smell. Old people. It smells like old people."

Claire stiffened in her seat. "Don't tell me what I like and what I don't like, Darrell."

Darrell's look of triumph faded from his face, and I briefly pondered putting Claire in charge of these meetings from now on. She obviously knew how to deal with obstinate men. How dare he call me old? He was ten years older than me. Asshole.

"It doesn't remind me of old people," offered George, who was in charge of local news. "Reminds me of my football days. I think that's why you," he pointed at Darrel, "said it reminded you of your college days. I'm sure both of us were slathered in it from time to time during football season."

Claire smiled at George and returned a nasty look in Darrell's direction. "I'm pretty sure Darrell still uses it, George. He's always whining about his old football injuries from his glory days. Must have been hard to be a backup quarterback."

I admired her skill. Earlier she had put him in his place. Now she was stomping what remaining ego he had left to pieces.

As much as I enjoyed it, I needed to refocus the group. "Now, Brenda, let's continue—"

"I've always loved the smell of cigarette smoke. I've never smoked in my life, but when I walk by a smoker outside, I inhale deeply. Does that count as a contact high?" Brenda directed her question to Claire, her best friend at the paper.

"I don't think you can get a contact high from cigarettes." Claire peeked at me out of the corner of her eyes, but it was so fleeting I didn't think anyone else noticed. Was I the only druggie she knew?

"Nail polish. I love the smell of nail polish," stated John.

Everyone, myself included, turned to stare at the director of classifieds. George asked, "Do you wear nail polish?" Without trying to look like he was being judgmental, George glanced at John's fingernails.

"N-no," stuttered John. "My wife changes her nail polish every night once she decides what outfit to wear at work the following day. She likes to coordinate the colors." He was cherry-red.

"Okay," I muttered. "Now that we have that settled, Brenda"—I snapped my fingers to get her to look at me and not at John's fingernails—"can we chat about circulation? How to drum up more online subscriptions?"

Brenda wiped the look of shock off her face and got down to business.

As the meeting winded down, Claire smiled at me triumphantly. I wasn't sure what the smile meant. The meeting was semi-productive at best, but I sensed it had to do with something else.

She was the last to leave the room, giving me the opportunity to ask, "What are you so happy about?"

"During the meeting I tweeted to ask followers what terrible smells they actually liked. Hundreds of people responded, and a few mentioned Bengay."

"What?"

Claire showed me her iPad confirming everything. "Wow." Avery wandered back into the room, realizing the meeting wasn't officially done. She tried to look professional about it, but I suspected she was snooping. Was she trying to figure out my relationship with Claire? I imagined her with an earpiece and mic like secret service agents have, reporting to Cora every second of the day.

I showed my assistant the iPad. "I think Claire's on to something. Get someone in Life to follow up with a story. And a list of advertisers who would want to sponsor the section, for online, not print," I instructed Avery before turning back to Claire. "Nice work. At least something came out of that meeting."

LATER THAT AFTERNOON, I waltzed into Claire's office without any fanfare. She yelped and dropped a book into her lap. Her department was almost deserted, and she probably wasn't expecting any visitors.

"It's only me, and I don't care if you're reading on the job," I said, sitting down in one of the chairs across from her desk. "What are you reading?" I massaged my stiff neck.

All traces of color slipped off her face, and for a moment I wondered if there was a pool of pink on the floor. This piqued my curiosity. "Don't tell me you're reading smut. Claire and smut—never would I have put those two together." I slapped my thigh.

She remained motionless.

"Are you okay? Do you need water or something?" I looked helplessly around the windowless room. Was she having a stroke?

"Y-yeah … I'm fine. You just startled me. That's all." She cleared her throat and went to drastic lengths to avoid eye contact.

Curious I stood and walked around her desk. Perching on the front of her desk I peered into her lap. When I saw the reason for her discomfort I had to smile. "Ah, this is a good book." I reached down and retrieved her copy of *Junkie* by William S. Burroughs.

"I'm so sorry," she confessed, nearly on the verge of tears.

"For what? Reading a book?" I knew why she felt guilty.

"No. Don't play with me. You know the reason."

"I do, and it's perfectly natural. If you thought I'd be mad or insulted, you're wrong. I can give you a list of books if you would like to read more."

Slowly, the color made its way back into her cheeks. "I just didn't want you to think I was judging you," she whispered.

"You're the last person I would think that of. Besides, the title really grabs your attention when looking for books on the subject." She looked away. I placed a hand on her shoulder. "I'm going for coffee. That swill in the break room won't cut it today. You want something from Starbucks?"

She nodded, and I decided to leave immediately to give her some time to recover.

I returned with my caramel macchiato and a cinnamon dolce latte for Claire. She still seemed distracted or hesitant to talk. "You can ask me questions, if you want."

She smiled guiltily. "It's just that I have no experience … with … this."

"With what? Drugs or addicts?"

"Both, really."

I nodded, unsure how to proceed. Was she having second thoughts about being in a relationship with me?

"Why'd you become an addict?"

I was in mid-swallow when she blurted the question, and I choked on the hot liquid. "What?" I attempted to clear my throat and then pounded on my chest. "No one, at least no one I know, sets out to be an addict." As I spoke, my voice got stronger and the burning tickle subsided. "At first it was fun. It made me feel good. And it helped me deal with life, stress, disappointments." I made a circular motion with my hand implying on and on. "It wasn't like I woke up one morning and said, 'You know, I want to be hooked on coke.' It was gradual. Snort a few lines here and there. The addiction didn't happen overnight—I know a lot of people think that. It was months in the making. And then, it took me months to recognize I had a problem. However, I wasn't ready to admit that really. Denial is powerful."

She tapped a pen on the cover of the book. "Have you ever done heroin?"

"Yes."

"With a needle?" Her face paled, and I wasn't sure if the reason was the image of a needle or the image of me shooting up heroin.

I nodded. I tried maintaining eye contact, but I broke it off. "Heroin wasn't my drug of choice. Coke was, but I dabbled with many drugs." I brushed a piece of lint off my pant leg. "I never did meth, though."

This relieved her some.

"And you've read this book?" She timidly held up the copy.

I wanted to laugh since I already insinuated I had, but I knew it was an uncomfortable situation for her. And I think she wanted to ask if I read it before or after I became hooked. I read it and many other books after I kicked my addiction. For the first few years, I read a lot of books to try to understand. And to cope.

But I wasn't in the mood to answer her question, so I veered toward a safer topic: a travel story.

"Many years ago, I was in New Orleans for work, but I managed to squeeze in some sightseeing. I love visiting authors' homes and landmarks. New Orleans is a wonderful place for book lovers. The Hotel Monteleone had many famous writers stay there, including William Faulkner, Anne Rice, Ernest Hemingway, Tennessee Williams, Truman Capote, Stephen Ambrose, and John Grisham."

Realizing I was getting off track completely, I continued with the initial story. "One afternoon I decided to visit William S. Burroughs's home"—I pointed to the book on her desk—"in Algiers, which is the town across the Mississippi River. It started off as a grand adventure, taking the ferry over. As soon as I stepped off the ferry, I found this delightful restaurant and had rice and beans and a couple of gin and tonics." I paused, feeling awkward. "It was before rehab of course, but at the time I wasn't using—well, not daily." I shrugged, knowing she wouldn't find that funny.

"The plan was to walk to Burroughs's home, which was on the outskirts. The sun was shining, albeit it was a chilly December day." I laughed. "All the locals kept apologizing that it was cold during my visit. Being from New York I thought they were crazy. I only had to wear long sleeves, but for them it was a travesty."

Claire smiled. Colorado winters had toughened her up as well.

"Then something awful happened. I was walking along this road and I saw a beat-up silver Ford Taurus cruising down the street, well over the speed limit for a residential area. I didn't think anything of it, until I heard the sound. The driver hit a dog, and I tell you, Claire, it was the most god-awful sound I ever heard. The dog's wailing." I rubbed the back of my neck, again. "Several people were on the sidewalk near the accident, and for some reason many of them turned to me. I had a camera strapped around my chest, and I thought for sure it screamed 'Tourist!' But in their helplessness they kept asking me to do something. Did I know the nearest vet? Was I a veterinarian? Everyone wanted to help the dog without going anywhere near the scene to see the poor creature."

"Did you?" Claire leaned forward in her chair, her eyes filled with anticipation.

I shook my head in shame and felt my throat close up. "No," I whispered. "I could never handle seeing animals suffer." I studied the top of the lid to my drink, focusing on the words to pull me out of my head so I wouldn't hear the dog. "Luckily, the dog's family was home and took the dog to the vet."

"Did the dog die?"

"I imagine so. It was three days before Christmas. Poor family."

We both remained quiet for a few moments. "Now when I think of Burroughs, I remember that day and it always puts me in a foul mood."

"I'm sorry, JJ."

I waved her concern away. "Don't worry about it. How could you have known? And his books are excellent."

"Did you see the house?"

"I did. It was a depressing, dilapidated home in this abandoned field. The whole day was a bust really. If you ever go to New Orleans, I suggest seeing Anne Rice's home. It's creepy, but it's a fun creepy. And it's in the Garden District—a much prettier part of Louisiana." I laughed.

She smiled, relieved that I'd returned to my jovial self.

"You know, I never told anyone about the dog before."

"I remember the time when you ran over a squirrel. God, you were so hard on yourself, even though there was nothing you could have done."

My eyes welled up. "I remember you telling me that the squirrel must have been suicidal and wanted to die because it darted right in front of me."

"I couldn't stand seeing you so upset." She smiled wanly. "You did use it to your advantage, though," Claire said.

I cocked my head, unsure where she was heading.

"Don't you remember that night? You asked me to stay with you since you were so distraught."

I burst into laughter. "That's right! Can you blame me? I was always looking for ways to get you in my bed."

"If I remember correctly, I held you all night."

"Yes, you did."

"I wonder what the people here would think if they knew that deep down you're a softy."

"Ha! Hopefully they don't find out, or I'll have people calling out every day claiming their hamster is on life support."

We both laughed, easing some of the tension from earlier. However, I did notice Claire watching my every move. I wondered if she thought I moved my hands in a certain way, indicating that I was an addict. Like flamboyant gay men with limp wrists. Or maybe I batted my eyes too much like I was in need of a fix.

She noticed that I was watching the way she was observing me, and she colored. Claire tapped the cover of *Junkie* and said, "What other books do you recommend?"

"Have you seen or read *Running with Scissors*?" She nodded. "He wrote another book called *Dry* and it's about his alcoholism. He did some drugs, but alcohol was his addiction."

She jotted down the title on her notepad. "What's the author's name?"

"Augusten Burroughs. I know it's slightly confusing considering you're reading William S. Burroughs. Maybe I should change my last name." I was hoping she'd laugh some, but her eyes looked sad. "I think you'll like *Dry*. It's a brutally honest book, and I should warn you, it can be a difficult read."

"Why difficult?"

"Throughout much of the book I hated him. His selfishness …"

"And?" Her voice was soft.

“And it really hit home and how selfish I had been. That’s one of the hardest parts to live with. Realizing how horrible I acted and all the things I did. I’m not even sure how to explain it, really. I think one has to live through an addiction to truly understand it. Not that I advocate that.” I lowered my eyes, knowing Claire wouldn’t find any irony in my statement.

“What’s the plan tonight?” I changed the subject. The work day was almost over, and Ian was spending the whole weekend with his grandparents at their cabin outside of Fort Collins near Horsetooth Reservoir.

chapter ten

"Morning, sunshine." Claire's perky voice was too animated for me at seven in the morning on a Saturday, especially since we'd been up most of the night.

"Pffft," was my not-so-clever reply.

"My, someone is grumpy this morning. Didn't sleep well?" She winked before pouring some coffee into a mug for me. "It's extra strong."

I took a tug. "Jesus! What is that? Jet fuel?" I sipped it again and felt life oozing back into my zombie form.

She smirked. Claire had a certain glow, and her messy bedhead was alluring.

"You look beautiful," I said over the rim of my cup, and then I swallowed as much as possible before I couldn't handle the taste any longer.

Claire leaned over the island countertop and mussed my hair. "You, on the other hand, have quite the bedhead today."

I patted the top of my hair, trying to tame the madness. I had unfortunate limp hair, making most hairdos impossible to maintain for longer than an hour. Years ago I opted to chop most of it off and to sport the short "messy" do. In the mornings though, the messy look was au naturel and out of control. And the amount of product I had to use to control the messy look complicated the next day look for sleepovers since it glued the chaos in unbecoming ways.

"And you are always commenting about Brenda's hair." She tsked. "If only she could see you now."

"Hey, at least I do something with it before I go to the office." My tone was defensive.

"She gets into the office hours before you." Claire was clearly enjoying this ribbing. It was turning me on.

I strutted over to the other side of the island. "Listen, don't push my buttons first thing in the morning." I playfully poked her shoulder with my finger.

"Or what?" She crossed her arms mischievously, which caused her robe to billow at the top and expose her breasts. I peeked down and saw she was completely naked.

"Or I'll have to do this." I kissed her forehead. "Or this." I worked down to her lips.

"Who are you punishing exactly?" she asked in a breathy voice.

"You." I undid her robe. Even with all the fucking we did the previous night, both of us were ready to pick up right where we left off. She started to walk off, presumably to the bedroom, but I pulled her back. I wanted to go down on her right there in the kitchen. I got down on my knees and peppered her thighs with soft kisses. I ran a finger along her pulsating, wet lips smiling that she was ready for me. I teased her with my tongue, and she let out a small gasp like she felt exposed in her kitchen but still wanted to continue no matter what.

I was more than happy to oblige. Rubbing my head between her legs, Claire laughed. "That should help your bedhead."

"My thinking exactly," I said, before inserting a finger and lapping her clit with my tongue.

"What in the hell do you think you're doing?" It was a male's voice.

Claire shrieked, "Darrell, what in the fuck are you doing here?"

She quickly wrapped her robe around her tightly like it was a suit of armor.

I heard something slam down on the countertop. "I've been trying to call you all night, but your phone is off. And I don't think your doorbell is working."

"So you barge into my home unannounced at this time of day."

"Oh, I knew you'd be up." I could picture him waving a hand in his condescending way. "I used the key in the fake rock." That must have been what he'd tossed onto the countertop.

I couldn't do anything since I was still between her legs. I had stopped what I was doing but had an impulse to keep going. I would love to get Claire off in front of Darrell without him knowing I was there. He'd probably always dreamed of having a threesome, and the idea that he wouldn't even know he was quasi-involved in one was almost too tempting.

"Why don't you have a seat and stop yelling at me?" I saw Claire motion to one of the barstools on the other side of the island. I think she wanted him to sit so he wouldn't be able to see me at all, hiding behind the island. I sat on the floor quietly and leaned against the cupboard. She grabbed an empty cup from the counter behind her and poured Darrell some of her jet fuel.

"Ballet, Claire. Ballet!"

This confused me. He'd barged into her house to discuss ballet. Darrell was off his rocker more than I suspected.

"Yes, Darrell. Ballet."

I looked up at Claire, completely baffled.

Was this their code word for fucking? Oral sex? Did he know someone was on the other side with Claire's juices all over her hair and face?

"You signed Ian up for ballet classes?" There was a loud thud, and I assumed he slammed his cup down on the granite top.

"Hey, don't break my cup or my counter, please."

He harrumphed.

"Ian wanted to take ballet classes, so I signed him up. You have a problem with that?" Her body tensed. "We both discussed Ian should partake in different types of activities. I didn't put up a fight when you signed him up for peewee football even though I wasn't happy about it." She stood over me in an attempt to hide me completely. Was she worried he would storm over to this side? Was he ever violent?

"You should have asked me first."

"Why? I'm paying for his classes. And you're paying for his football. I don't need your permission to spend my money."

"You do when it involves my son."

"Oh, really." Her voice told me she was ready to battle him to the end.

"Do I need to call you every time I run to the store for food? When I take him clothes shopping? You are being completely ridiculous and a fucking asshole, I might add."

I wanted to high-five her. Actually I wanted to lick her. Her robe billowed around me and her legs were spread wide open in my face. I could smell her, and it was intoxicating.

"Claire," Darrell whispered. "Think about what you're doing."

"And what's that?"

"We don't want to encourage certain types of behavior."

"Dancing." I couldn't see her face but was fairly certain she was staring him down, daring him to say what he really meant.

"You know what I mean."

"Yes I do, and it's asinine. Are you implying if Ian was gay you wouldn't love him anymore?"

"What?" He paused. "Of course not. But I don't think we should encourage him to be … that."

"Encourage." She laughed. "It's not something you can foster, Darrell. People are born straight, gay, bisexual, transgendered ... Signing Ian up for ballet won't turn him gay."

"Bisexual," he scoffed.

"What? You don't think people can be attracted to both sexes. You know I've been in relationships with women."

I thought I could hear him grinding his teeth. "I wouldn't consider you bi, though."

"Really? Why? Because we have a son together?"

I was tempted to jump up and shout "Surprise!" Claire squeezed her legs against my head, and I wondered if she knew what I was thinking. But all thoughts of Darrell left my head and I licked her clit. She knocked my head with both her knees and kept them in place, preventing me from trying anything further. However, she quickly glanced down, and I saw she couldn't wait for Ian's father to leave. Did fighting turn her on? I made a note to remember that for the future.

"Listen, I came to discuss Ian and ballet. I won't stand for it."

"Too late. I paid for the classes in full, and Ian likes it. Besides he has a crush on one of the girls in his class and has asked her out on a playdate for next weekend."

"Really?" The hopefulness in Darrell's voice annoyed me. "His first date."

"I don't think we can really call it that. They have plans to fly kites together." Claire leaned toward the counter again, and once again my face was right in her honey spot. "Did you ever think your son was smarter than you? He's the only boy in the whole class and already has one girl gaga over him."

Darrell giggled, and I wanted to puke. That man should never giggle. And he was worried that his son was a fag?

"He's a regular Casanova," he said.

I felt the smile in his voice.

"Now, can you please apologize and go. I have things I need to do today."

I heard him stand. "Fine, whatever. Have a nice day." The sound of his retreating footsteps and then the closing of the front door was a relief.

"What an ass!" Claire gripped her coffee, and I saw the whites of her knuckles. Her nostrils flared.

"Do you two fight like that all the time?"

She shook her head. "No, but when we do, it involves parenting Ian. He thinks I'm too liberal, and I worry he's too much of a stick-in-the-mud. Darrell's not always like that. He didn't throw a fit when Ian wanted a Barbie."

"Really?"

"He actually bought Ian a Barbie Dream Car. Of course, Darrell also got him a G.I. Joe."

"Then why is he throwing a fit about ballet, then?"

"If I had to guess, it has something to do with his ex-wife. She still pops into the picture, and when she does, Darrell lashes out at those he can. It can be infuriating."

I leaned against the far counter, sipping my coffee. "You may not want to hear this right now, but you're damn sexy when you're mad."

The color started to return to her knuckles as I watched the strain ebb from her body. "Really?" She quirked an eyebrow and brushed some hair out of her eyes.

"What things do you have to do today?" I asked.

"What?" She raised her eyebrows.

"You told Darrell you had things you had to do today. What?" I shrugged.

"You."

This brought a smile to my lips and a warm sensation down below. "You have to do me?" I made my voice as appealing as possible. It worked. With a simple hand motion she undid the ties of her robe. I could see the wetness on her legs glistening from my earlier efforts.

I moved to kiss her, but she placed a delicate finger on my lips, pushing me back. Shaking her head, she said, "I'm in charge, now."

Her confidence made my clit ache for her. "What do you plan on doing to me?" I whispered in heady excitement.

Not saying a word or letting any emotion cross her face, she grabbed my hand and led me upstairs to her bedroom. The sheets were a tangled mess from our earlier escapades, and the room smelled of blissful sex.

She turned me so my back was facing her and reached around to undo my robe, letting it flutter to the floor. "On the bed," she demanded, but before I could respond, she pushed me gently onto my stomach. I felt her wetness on my ass and let out a whimper of desire.

Claire traced the outline of my tattoo, and it took me a second to realize she was using her erect nipple. Her hair cascaded over my back, and it was like her silky strands had a direct connection to my pulsing bud, sending shockwaves. No woman had ever turned me on this much through the simple act of touching.

Delicately she kissed my back and moved up to nibble on my ear. I turned my head, and she sensed I needed her lips on mine. She kissed me frantically, plunging her tongue deep into my mouth and just as quickly she stopped, focusing on my tattoo again. Every lick and nip sent a new wave of emotion. This wasn't just an orgasm in the making; she was helping heal my soul.

She continued to focus on my back, so I wasn't expecting it when I felt her fingers spreading my lips, pleading for permission to enter. I could feel my wetness envelop her, and she plunged in deeply.

I let out a gasp, which excited her more. Frantically, she moved her fingers in and out, bringing me to the brink. The fireworks started to form behind my lids, and I squeezed my eyes tightly not to miss the show.

That's when Claire decided to stop the performance and rolled me over onto my back. Straddling me again, I felt her juices mixing with mine. She lowered her clit onto mine and moved ever so slightly. Sighing, I reached up and traced a finger along each breast before teasing one of her nipples. She reached down with her hand and started to rub her own clit.

"Oh, fuck," I moaned.

Overcome with desire I tried to enter her. Slapping my hand away she raised an eyebrow, commanding me to watch. With her free hand she slid two of her fingers into her own pussy. I cried out as if she had just entered me.

My eyes bulged, and I had to grip the sheets tightly with both hands to stop myself from interfering. Claire wanted to be in charge, and I didn't want to mess with her plans. She arched her back, tossing her head even farther back and groaned loudly. Her hand moved in and out forcefully as she bounced up and down on my pelvis. Opening her mouth she let out the most satisfying shriek I had ever heard any woman belt out, and her body pulsed. Wave after wave. Yet she didn't let up. Her stamina was astounding, and my restraint melted.

I practically threw Claire onto her back and climbed on top. This time she didn't stop me. Covering her mouth with mine as if I wanted to consume her orgasm, I slipped my fingers inside her. She was still in the middle of coming and squirted all over my hand. The warmth pulled me in deeper, and I felt her legs tightening, holding me in and not wanting to let me go.

I never wanted to let her go.

Never.

Claire's entire body rocked, and her fingers dug deep into my back.

Not wanting this to be the end, but to be the beginning, I moved down and took her swollen lips into my mouth gently, making sure she wasn't over stimulated. I wanted her to come again, but not too quickly or hard. Her moan told me to proceed, slowly. That was perfectly fine with me. I could spend a lifetime between her legs and not feel completely sated.

My tongue slid along the inside of her lips, and I entered her a little. Her taste was sensually overwhelming; I had to move down to explore her inner thigh so I wouldn't come just from swallowing her juices. I kept moving down as my mouth explored her lower legs before I sucked on each of her delicate toes. Claire watched me with such fervent intensity that I decided to tease her some and placed her foot near my clit. With her big toe she circled my bud, bringing me back to the brink quickly. Stopping her with my own commanding look, I dropped her foot and entered her with my tongue again.

Deeper and deeper I went.

Her back arched, and her hips urged me further inside.

I knew she was close and needed release. I lapped her clit and entered her with a finger.

"Please," she begged.

It was time. I pushed inside as far as she wanted and concentrated on her clit. Her fingers clutched at my hair, and she scored my scalp with her nails. When she started to come her upper body bolted upright, and she gripped my back with both hands. It took everything I had not to stop and scream out in ecstasy. I held my finger and tongue in place as the orgasm coursed through her body. Her convulsions shook the bed, and she collapsed back.

For several minutes I kept my face buried in her pussy, inhaling her smell. Finally, I was home.

Eventually, she pulled me up and I lay on top of her. Running her fingers through my hair, Claire said, "I'm sorry."

"What are you sorry for?" I was too spent to look into her eyes.

"I think I drew blood on your back and ruined your tattoo," she whispered.

"Trust me, you wouldn't be able to ruin it or anything. Never."

Her body stiffened. "But I did. God, I did."

I pushed up and propped my head on my hand. "What are you talking about, Claire? This was wonderful. Absolutely wonderful."

"But I pushed you away that night." She closed her eyes, squeezing out one tiny tear.

"What? Oh, that night." I placed my hand tenderly on her cheek. "Don't think of it like that. We're together now. That's all that matters."

"You scared me that night. Never before had I felt so loved." She let out a sad laugh. "You'd think that would be a good thing. But you loved me completely, and that scared me. I was so young. And stupid. All those wasted years. So many years."

"Shhh." I rested my finger on her velvet lips. "Don't think of it like that. Besides, you'd never want to go back and change it. Ian. You love your son. You'd never want to change that."

Her eyes agreed.

"We can torture ourselves to the end of days thinking what if. Let's not do that to each other. Now. That's what matters."

She answered by kissing me sweetly. "I have always loved you, even when you were so far away."

"Me too, Claire. Me too."

Claire made love to me like someone determined to show through her touches that I was the only person she wanted or ever wanted.

By mid-morning we both drifted off to sleep, with her in my arms.

chapter eleven

My morning didn't start off well. First, I slept through my alarm. So did Claire. However, both of us liked to get to work early, so sleeping in meant I didn't leave her house until a little after seven. The nights I spent at her house, I rode my bike instead of running to avoid anyone noticing the same car parked outside. Claire offered to give me a lift, but it was one of those stunning Colorado mornings. The sky was a brilliant blue, yet the air was brisk. Just what I needed to jumpstart my brain.

As I locked my bike up outside of the office, Darrell rode up next to me on a Trek. From the looks of the bike, it was brand-spanking new.

"Morning, Darrell." I tried not to think of the last time I saw him so I wouldn't get a goofy grin on my face. Actually, I hadn't seen him since I was between Claire's legs.

"Morning." He busied himself by locking up his Trek.

"New bike?" I asked.

"Yeah." He looked up after snapping his U-lock. I saw him eye my Specialized Vita Pro that I'd dropped a couple grand on soon after moving to Denver. His Trek wasn't cheap by any means. "My son wants to go riding in the mountains this summer."

For a moment, I forgot all about our troubles and smiled at Darrell. "Sounds wonderful."

He shrugged. It wasn't the most heartfelt exchange, but it felt good not to have an acrimonious discussion for once.

"Catch you later, Darrell."

From inside the glass door, I saw Darrell pull out his cell phone. I was able to catch the beginning of the conversation after I edged the door open some.

"Guess what your old man just did, Ian?" Darrell was smiling broadly.

With that, I left, not wanting to intrude on the father-son moment. Maybe he wasn't such an ass.

After showering in my private bathroom, I sat in my office with wide-eyed and crazy-haired Brenda and Avery. "I put this …" Brenda waved a paper in the air and then held it close to her face, scrutinizing it with squinted eyes. I wondered if she knew she was holding her glasses in her left hand. "What is this?"

"Report?" I offered, tilting my head, baffled by this woman.

The crazy woman shook her head. "No. This?" She tapped the paper with her glasses.

"Spreadsheet," said Avery, unsure if she was helping or insulting Brenda.

"Spreadsheet. Yes, spreadsheet!" Brenda looked up triumphantly.

And this was the woman in charge of circulation. No wonder our subscribers were fleeing faster than rats on a sinking ship.

My phone rang. "JJ Cavendish." Usually I didn't answer during a meeting, but I needed a diversion from the Brenda circus.

"JJ," Claire whispered. "I need you."

"Now?"

"Yes!"

I set the phone down. "I'm needed in the pressroom. I'll be right back. Carry on."

Brenda and Avery nodded, not caring. Brenda was usually clueless about her surroundings, and Avery was studying the woman like she was trying to determine if Brenda was for real or if she was putting on a show.

I rushed down the back steps and knocked on Claire's door.

"JJ?"

"Yes," I responded, baffled why she didn't say come in.

"Come in, but make sure you close the door."

I followed her directions. "What's going on?"

"I had a little accident." She turned around and her boobs were bulging out of her bra. Her shirt was completely unbuttoned.

"I was in a meeting." I was tempted to cancel the meeting and whisk her off to a hotel.

"I'm not trying to seduce you," she whispered. "I tore my shirt on the file cabinet." She looked around like she expected some of our photographers to pop out and say cheese.

I burst into laughter.

"It's not funny." She tried not to laugh. "Okay, it is. But I can't go out there like this." She pointed to her tits. This wasn't the type of office one could strut around in a red lace bra. I tried to imagine an office where you could. Paris, maybe? Amsterdam?

I had to sit down. I was laughing so hard. "This would only happen to you."

Darrell burst into the room. "Claire, you can't have page three in the local sec—"

It took him that long to notice that her shirt was ripped open. I jumped up to block his view.

"Shut the door, Darrell," ordered Claire.

"What in the hell is going on in here?" He looked to me and then tried to see Claire over my shoulder.

"I called JJ to help me. I tore my shirt on the file cabinet." She covered her breasts with her arms but held them too tightly, and it made them bulge out even more.

"And you called JJ? Not Brenda?" he asked, dumbfounded.

Claire gave him a not-right-now shake of the head.

I yanked my sweater off and handed it to her and motioned for Darrell to turn around. He did. Even the back of his neck was red from embarrassment. How in the world had these two ever slept together? Immediately, I regretted thinking that and had to think of my happy place on the beach to erase the image.

With more dignity than I would have been able to muster in the situation Claire said, "I need B3, Darrell."

"Put the ad on four in the main section," he demanded.

"I can't. The ad is full color and three is the designated color spot, which already has a half-page full color. It can't go on two, four, or five—they only support spot color, not full. The front and back pages are full color but are out of the question, obviously."

"Dammit, Claire. Advertising doesn't dictate where we put the news."

"Actually, it does. Our diagrammer lays out the paper every day, and you work around the ads. Tomorrow's paper is no different."

"Not this time."

I was amazed by their back and forth. Claire obviously wasn't disturbed that Darrell just saw her tits.

"Put the color ad in the sports section."

Claire rolled her eyes. "There's a full-page car ad in the sports section. I can't put a furniture ad in the fucking sports section. The advertiser would have a shit fit."

"All right. The classified section then."

"Can't." She didn't even bother to explain why. Not that it mattered. From the look on Darrell's face he wasn't listening to her.

"Why do you need B3?" I asked.

"We have a local expose that needs an entire page, and it needs to go in the local section. Page two is out with the obits and everything, and four is half-filled with ads."

"Fine, put it on five."

Both looked at me. Darrell couldn't believe I said it, and Claire looked unsure but not against the idea.

"Look, we have the stock page on five, and it's totally useless in today's world. I've been meaning to kill it when the time was right, and I think this is the right time. Put something on the front page mentioning that the stock page is finito."

"JJ, the stock page has been on page five for decades. You can't just kill it." Darrell tried keeping his voice calm, like he was talking to a child who was desperate to enter the lion pit at the zoo.

"And by the time most of our readers see it, the stock market is already open, and all the prices listed are completely useless information. I'm killing it and giving the space to you, Darrell. Consider it my gift."

"And how do you propose we fill it every day?" he asked through gritted teeth.

"Catchy local stories, of course." I smiled sweetly. "And if we don't have enough, we can fill the space with ads." I turned to Claire. "I know that will kill the house ad budget for a bit, but I think it will help in the long run. Tell your reps to really push for clients to purchase more spots in the local section since we are jazzing it up. And it's another page for black and white and spot ads for the diagrammer to work with. I've noticed that B2 and B4 have had some weird stacking of smaller ads on top of larger ads for the past few weeks that resemble a tottering half-pyramid or something. I don't like it."

Claire conceded, but remained quiet.

Darrell gave me one last glare before storming back upstairs.

"I'm starting to think he really doesn't like you," said Claire.

"Really? He hides it so well." I closed Claire's door, and she gave me a confused look before looking down to ensure she was covered, even though she had put on my sweater moments earlier. I locked her door this time.

She quirked an eyebrow.

I kissed her and was surprised that she didn't offer any resistance. "Can you manage to have a wardrobe malfunction every day?"

"Does it turn you on?"

"Yes it does. How soundproof are these walls?"

"Not very." She gasped slightly when I unzipped her pants and let them fall. I then lowered her panties.

"You'll have to be very quiet," I advised.

"You can't be serious." Her voice wasn't convincing at all.

"You don't think so." I got on my knees. "Do you want me to stop?"

Claire was conflicted.

"The door's locked, and Avery thinks I'm in the pressroom. Most of your staff is on sales calls." I flicked her clit with my tongue, and Claire's resolve disappeared. I slid my tongue between her lips, entering her. Claire let out a silent sigh.

It didn't take long for her to become wet, and I inserted a finger. Then a second and third. Claire was doing her best to stay quiet. Leaving my fingers inside her, I stood to kiss her and keep her from moaning. I increased the intensity of moving my fingers in and out and went as far into her as possible. When she started to quiver, I held her head against my chest with my free arm to muffle the sounds. She bit through my shirt into my shoulder, and I knew it would leave a mark.

"I can't believe we did that." She sat on her desk motionless, with her pants still around her ankles.

I smiled. "I probably should get back to my office to prepare for the big visit next week."

She nodded with this wonderful, naughty schoolgirl grin and pulled up her pants. Before I left I whispered, "You're beautiful, Claire. Can I take you to dinner tonight?"

Claire softly kissed my cheek. "Yes. You can do whatever you want with me."

chapter twelve

Cora stood at the podium in front of the entire staff. The room was abuzz. This was the first time any CEO of the company had visited the Denver office since Beale Media Corp purchased the paper back in the eighties. Before everything had been done via videoconference. On rare occasions, people, such as Darrell, were ordered to New York for meetings. Being summoned to New York was not a good thing, and most avoided it if at all possible.

"JJ has told me how hard all of you are working to turn this paper around." Cora leaned on the podium. "I have to be honest. One year ago, I didn't have high hopes for this branch. We talked about closing the doors and focusing our resources elsewhere. Then JJ, in her bold style, said, 'Give me a year. I'll turn it around.'" Cora looked to me as I stood bashfully on the side of the stage. She and I both knew I never asked for this post. "Well, there's a reason we call her the Miracle Girl." She winked at me in a way so everyone could see it.

Many people started to clap. I winced when Cora said it, even though I had been mentally preparing for it all day. I locked eyes on Claire. She shook her head before staring at Cora. I chuckled at the intensity of Claire's gaze. Luckily the lights on the stage shielded Cora from seeing the audience, safeguarding Claire from unwanted attention. Staring at the CEO like she wanted to use Cora's head as a bowling ball wasn't the best way of being noticed.

"The war isn't over," Cora continued once the clapping subsided. "But the first major battle is a resounding victory." She flipped on the PowerPoint presentation that Avery and I had slaved over for the past week, showing the increase in Twitter followers, the increase in blog visits, and a slight increase in circulation numbers. The bump in online advertising was the biggest change.

"The biggest increases are due to Avery's blogger competition." Cora motioned to Kung Fu Avery and encouraged people to applaud. "And Darrell's new Daily Dose of Junk News." Cora gestured to Darrell.

Darrell looked uncomfortable with the recognition, and I enjoyed seeing him squirm in his seat, accepting the approbation with as much decorum as he was willing to show. The Junk News reports went against his moral fiber, yet he wasn't fool enough to clear the air and say it was my idea. Darrell, like most newspapermen, yearned for attention.

AFTER CORA'S TALK, Bill whisked her into the crowd for the usual meet and greet. Unlike me, Cora loathed this part of these meetings. She was not a people person. While we managed to stay friends after Cora became CEO, most of Cora's coworkers who were also her friends couldn't get over the change in Cora. She became no-holds-barred when it came to business. I admired that about her. Others thought their friendship should come first. One friend was floored when Cora let her go right after coming back from maternity leave. The woman's temp had proven her merit, and Cora didn't hesitate one bit when making the decision. If she knew why I hadn't fired Darrell yet, she would have my head on a platter. Personal feelings should never be a factor.

I stepped in to help ease Cora's burden. "Cora, allow me to introduce you to some of the staff." Only a handful of eager beavers lunged forward to meet the CEO. The other workers who really didn't care about working their asses off and getting promotions headed straight for the food, beer, and wine.

When I introduced Claire, Cora smiled genuinely. "Ah, Claire, I've heard so much about you—all the changes you've implemented."

"JJ has been such an inspiration and has lit a fire under us." Claire's eyes beamed when she turned toward me and then back to my boss.

Cora looked to me, and then back to Claire. I could see her making connections that I wasn't all that comfortable with.

"JJ does have a way with *some* people."

Claire missed her meaning. "Oh, that she does."

Cora's lips thinned, and Bill saw a chance to whisk her out of the room. He knew better than most that Cora's niceness was short-lived and not to push his luck. As he guided Cora by me, he nudged my shoulder with his, which was Bill's way of saying way to go. I was fairly certain what the nudge meant, but I was hoping both Cora and Bill didn't see the look in Claire's eyes and mine for that matter.

Everyone who had surrounded Cora in hopes of making an impression scurried off to the food tables.

Claire turned to me and whispered, "That's the mysterious Cora, then."

"Yep. Meet and greets aren't really her thing."

"I gathered. Does she know about us?" Claire leaned in so no one could hear.

I shook my head, unsure of who I was trying to convince: her or me. "I better get upstairs for the 'real' meeting." I made quote marks in the air and shrugged.

The real meeting wasn't as positive as the show earlier. The numbers confirmed that the battle was much harder than anticipated. After Bill left when we finished our powwow, Cora insisted that I join her for a late dinner. Bill was already on the way to the airport for a San Francisco visit to do some damage control at one of our largest papers, but Cora's husband and kid were meeting her for a week in Vail the following day. Her husband loved hiking and mountain biking. That was the real reason why she'd come to Colorado. Not to rally the troops, but to have a much-needed holiday.

"So, JJ, how are you liking the West? Is there enough to keep your interest?" Cora's penetrating green eyes unnerved me. She knew something.

I had a feeling Cora was hinting about my personal life. "I'm liking it just fine." I motioned to the waiter for another tea. I was battling a sore throat, and all I wanted was to take a hot bath and curl up in bed with Claire, which wasn't going to happen since Ian was home.

"Is that because of Claire?" Cora sipped her wine and peered at me over the rim of her glass.

I smiled. Cora always had a way of knowing things without being told. "Maybe." My cold made my voice sound like the jazz singer, Louis Armstrong.

"She's your *best* friend from your college days, right? I knew there was a reason you didn't fight me too much when I wanted to send you here. You put up a fight, but not the rational fight you're capable of when you really don't want to do something."

I didn't confirm or deny it.

Cora's smile indicated the jig was up. "Well, is she the reason you're liking it here?"

"I wasn't aware that Claire worked for the paper until my first day."

"I bet that was a shock for you." Cora tittered. The wine was going to her head, or maybe it was Denver's thin air that made her more susceptible to getting tipsy. "But you still had an inkling she was in Colorado. Am I right?"

I ignored the comment. I had never told her that I was in love with Claire, and I had no plan to tell her now.

"Come now. You can't possibly think you can stay here. In this town." Cora waved dramatically. "Not you. You love excitement. Adventure. Culture. God, what do Coloradoans do for fun? Cow pie tossing contests?"

"I did grow up here," I said through gritted teeth. "It's not the middle of nowhere. We even have an art museum that's one of the largest between Chicago and the West Coast."

"Yes, I saw that article in your paper this morning. Nice piece. I especially loved that the initials of the Denver Art Museum spell: DAM. As in DAM, how did I end up here?"

I hated it when Cora was in a combative mood about trifling matters that were of no concern to her. I suspected it had more to do with Cora's job. Rumors were she wouldn't be CEO much longer and she needed a whipping girl to boost her ego. While the Denver paper was improving somewhat, three others folded in the past six months. It looked like mine would be next.

There was an awkward silence. My tea arrived, and I blew into it immediately to stay busy.

"She has a kid, doesn't she? Claire, I mean."

"How many spies do you have?"

"You of all people know the answer to that." Cora flashed a knowing smile. "Do you think you can play family? Don't get me wrong." She set her glass down and looked like the old Cora I loved. "I want to see you settled down and not—well, we don't need to rehash that. But settle down here? I can count the skyscrapers on one hand."

She must have sensed my ire that I was desperately trying to tame.

"Don't get mad. I just want to make sure you're happy. I still care about you. I always will."

I nodded.

"You know this move was meant to be a stepping stone, right? Does Claire know that? Yes, you may be here for a couple of years if the paper doesn't close, but eventually you'll be back in New York. They're grooming you for CEO."

I started to speak.

Cora waved me off. "It's no secret I'm on my way out. And I'm okay with that. I'm ten years older than you, and to be honest, I'm exhausted. This business sucks the life out of you. But it also gets into your blood. Do you really want to throw away the chance of running the whole shebang and live here in Denver?"

Before I could stop myself I said, "I ran away from Claire once before. It was a horrible mistake that haunts me to this day. I don't plan on doing it again."

Cora sat back, with her wineglass pressed against her chest. "So she's the one, then? The one that broke your heart?"

I bristled.

"You don't have to answer. I can see it in your face. Before you get in over your head, don't get too involved until you know you can do it for the long haul. It's not fair to Claire or to her child."

Before moving back home, I wouldn't have considered giving up my ambition to be the top dog of Beale Media Corp. But now, with Claire in the picture, I wasn't so sure that was what I wanted.

Cora raised her hand to get the waiter's attention and then ordered two slices of cheesecake and another hot tea with honey for me, since I had sucked down half of my most recent cup.

"You still having issues with your neck?"

I rubbed it. "Sometimes."

She shook her head. "You work too hard, but I know you won't stop. Besides, I need you to." Her sweet smile put me at ease. And then she pounced. "Why haven't you fired Darrell yet?"

I choked on the remnants of my lukewarm tea. "Why?" I tried playing stupid.

"Why? Because the guy sucks at his job." She flipped her hand in the air to emphasize the truth. "And I don't believe for one second that he thought of the Daily Dose of Junk News. I have to admit, though, that was a nice touch sticking him with it to shut him up. I heard you threatened to fire him in front of everyone and, if I remember correctly, that was the plan." She tapped her manicured fingernails on the table.

"You're little spy has been busy. Is it Avery?" I finished the tea to make room for the next cup.

Cora pasted on her poker face, and I knew I'd never get the truth out of her.

"I don't think firing Darrell will help morale much," I defended, knowing it was a pathetic attempt. Getting rid of Mr. Negativity would greatly help morale.

"Uh-huh. If you have one more run-in with him, you have to fire him. Or that won't be good for your authority. Come on. I trained you better than this. Colorado is making you soft."

"Is that an order?" I grimaced.

"Yes. It is." Cora fixed me with a stare. "Are we clear?"

"Crystal."

She placed a hand on mine, and I was surprised by its warmth. "You're doing a great job here, and I'm proud of you. Just don't go soft on me. People are saying good things about you back home. Don't blow it."

chapter thirteen

The last Sunday in May was beautiful at eighty degrees and not a cloud in sight. My parents invited me over for a barbeque, and I brought Claire and Ian.

I think my parents always suspected my feelings for Claire in the past, but they never asked. It was like all of us went to great lengths to avoid the subject. The subject was too painful for me, and they probably understood. Whenever they'd filled me in about people I knew, they never mentioned Claire. Pops hadn't even told me she worked at the paper.

"It's good to have a child running around in the yard again, isn't it dear?" My mother turned to my father, smiling wistfully.

Pops nodded enthusiastically. "Maybe Claire will let him come over, and we can pretend he's our grandchild." My father nudged my arm, letting me know he was giving me a hard time.

Claire and I hadn't told anyone that we were a couple, but I was happy to hear that they liked having Ian around. I planned on having him over a lot in the future. A child couldn't have enough grandparents in my opinion.

"It's not too late for JJ to have a child," said Claire.

"You've got to be kidding. I'm forty-four."

"Forty-five, dear," corrected my mother. The barbeque was part of my birthday celebrations. I had already warned Ian and Claire that there wouldn't be a cake since my family always went to the local diner for pie after most meals. Ian was taken with the idea.

"Good point, Mom. I'm forty-five."

Claire looked at me with an expression I couldn't decipher. "I've always wanted to adopt a child," said Claire as she watched her son buzz around the yard chasing a soccer ball that he kicked wildly about in some type of game only he understood. "You could adopt."

"You've always wanted to adopt a child?" I couldn't hide the shock in my tone or keep it off my face.

"Jesus, JJ, you could have tried to disguise your surprise," said Claire as she bit into her hot dog, smearing ketchup and mustard on her chin. After chewing she added, "I thought you were a crack newspaper woman." I handed her a napkin and motioned to her chin.

My father chuckled. "Newspapers are in her blood, and trust me when I say JJ can keep a secret."

Claire's eyebrows shot up.

"I can see by your expression, Claire, that I'm right. Must be a good one." He looked to me. "Will the story break soon?" He sipped his Coke.

Relief flooded through me. He thought I had breaking news.

I smiled and took a much larger bite than I intended out of my burger.

But my mom wasn't ready to ignore the thread Claire introduced. "Would you ever adopt a child, JJ?"

I let out a puff of air. "The idea has crossed my mind. But …" I looked toward Ian. "How would I juggle work and a child?"

Claire answered for my mom. "Find a partner who would like to quit her job and be a stay-at-home mom."

Not thinking, I said, "Is that something you want?"

"I always wanted to stay home with Ian. Being a single mom wouldn't allow it."

"But now, you could give up your job and raise children?"

I saw my parents watching us with great interest.

"I would jump at the chance." Claire fixed her eyes on mine, and I knew that was what she wanted. The idea didn't terrify me. It appealed to me more than I ever thought it would. Could I finally have a normal life? Married with kids and have happiness?

My father cleared his throat. "So, JJ, are you willing to let us in on one secret?"

My mother shushed him, but Claire turned to him and said, "I'm not sure about JJ, but I have no issues telling you I'm madly in love with your daughter."

He slapped his hand on the picnic table. "Hot damn! Does that mean I can start taking Ian to see the Rockies this summer?"

I had never heard my father utter any curse word before.

Claire smiled broadly at me. "He would love it."

My father pulled out his phone. "I can get tickets for all of us next Saturday. Does that work?"

"Sure, Pops. Sounds good to me."

LATER THAT NIGHT, after dropping Ian off at his dad's so they could spend Memorial Day together, Claire and I returned to her house.

"Have you been with many women?" I lay on my back with my head on Claire's taut stomach. It amazed me that a woman who gave birth was in such amazing shape at our age. I was a runner and a biker, so staying slim was easy for me. Claire was devoted to yoga, and it wasn't until I saw her naked that I realized yoga was more than connecting to a higher consciousness. It was a rigorous workout, and Claire's body proved it.

Claire played with my pubic hair, not in an attempt to arouse me but because she seemed to like the feel of running her fingers through the course patch. We had spent the previous hour making love and were now enjoying each other's company without the built-up sexual tension. "Not many after you. Not many men either." She propped her head up on a pillow. "There was this one woman I had an intense relationship with when I turned thirty."

"Intense. That sounds interesting."

"At first it was. Adrian was beautiful, intelligent, and funny. I really thought I could settle down with her. But she also had this mysterious side. It was exciting. She would meet me for lunch and instead we would slip off to the nearest hotel. If we had sex at my place she was usually gone when I woke in the morning, but there was always a gift. A rose, a card, chocolates, or something small, and it always put a smile on my face.

"Then I realized we never went back to her place. She said she was embarrassed by it and preferred my house. That struck me as odd since she was a successful corporate attorney who was a few years older than me. All of the mystery started to fade away, and I suspected I was in a relationship with a married woman."

"Get out!"

"That's what I thought. When confronted, she laughed and said how in the world would she find the time to have a husband and a lover with her schedule? I believed her. I wanted to, so I did. The months slipped by and, as the holidays approached I noticed she had less and less time for me.

"Then one night the paper held a Christmas bash at a swanky hotel and so did Adrian's company on the same night. That's when I bumped into her and her husband."

I sat up. "Did you say anything?"

"Nope. Adrian introduced me as a friend. That was the last time I saw her."

"Scandalous! She's lucky, really."

"What in the world does that mean?"

"You're in advertising. It wouldn't have crossed your mind to expose her."

"Oh, really. Are you saying if it was you, you'd out her in the paper?"

"It would be really tempting to do so. As Darrell likes to say I'm a muckraker at heart. No morals at all."

"So do I have to worry?" She raised an eyebrow confidently.

"Don't break my heart." I kissed her before she had a chance to respond. "And no, I would never do anything to hurt you."

"You better not. I don't put up with shit anymore."

"Noted. Do you put up with this?" I peppered the hollow of her throat with delicate kisses.

"Hmmm … if done correctly."

"Well, you let me know if I need to try again. I have all the time in the world."

"Any chance you can stop by my office for an appointment on Tuesday, say around lunch?"

I looked up. "Sure. Is everything all right?"

"Whoa! You slip into boss mode pretty quickly." I felt the color rush to my face. "I was hoping for a private meeting," she said.

It wasn't until she winked at me suggestively that I realized what she meant. "Oh, that. Shit, we can set up those meetings every day. And I love seeing the adventurous side of you, Ms. Nicholls."

"What about my other side?"

Puzzled, I asked, "What do you mean?"

"What we talked about earlier? Being a mom?"

I couldn't stop the smile from spreading across my face. "Before I came home—"

"To me," she interrupted.

"Yes, before I came home to you, I wouldn't have considered it."

"What?"

"Having a family."

She sat up in bed and held my chin in her hand. "And now?"

I kissed her. "And now, I'm considering it."

TWO DAYS LATER I approached Claire's office and said, "Are you ready for our—?"

Brenda sat across from Claire, and her head whipped around.

"Our meeting," Claire finished for me since I was sure my face was turning red, considering the prickly sensation I felt. Even though I didn't say anything damning in front of Brenda, a wave of unease gripped my body. And why did it have to be Brenda—the biggest office gossip?

Brenda made no effort to clear the room. "JJ, I'm glad to see you. Maybe you can use your magical skills to help me get to the bottom of this."

Letting out a long breath to steady my heart I said, "What's going on?"

"Claire here won't tell me who her new beau is." Brenda grinned conspiratorially.

Beau. Did she really just say beau?

I turned my face to Claire. "I didn't know you were seeing someone."

Claire clenched her mouth and sucked in her lips to keep her cool. After calming herself she responded, "That's because I'm not."

"Oh, please. You've been mooning about this place for weeks. And look at you!" Brenda waved a finger.

Claire looked down at her outfit, and I studied her.

Brenda let out a frustrated sigh. "Since when do you come to work dressed like that?"

That's when I noticed Claire wore a blouse with a plunging neckline and her makeup was more prevalent. I stood and motioned for Brenda to follow me behind Claire's desk. "Look at those heels and stockings. I can never get the line so straight in the back." I wanted to run my hand up the back of her toned leg.

"What about the skirt? It's short, tight, and sexy," Brenda added, tugging on it. Claire slapped her hand away.

"Yes, I agree." I sat on the edge of Claire's desk and crossed my arms. "She makes a convincing case. Tell us who you're seeing."

Claire held a red pen in her hand, and I thought for sure she was going to snap it in two, imagining it was my neck. She refused to speak.

"Come on, Claire. It's just us." Brenda motioned to me like we had been best friends since kindergarten.

"Yeah. Tell us."

"I—" Claire stopped, shook her head, and laughed.

"Oh, is it someone we work with? Is that why you dressed up today?" asked Brenda, hitting too close to home for me. Eventually our relationship would surface, but I didn't want it to so early for Claire's sake. Sleeping with the boss could be construed in unsavory ways.

"Brenda, if you'll excuse us, JJ and I have a meeting." Her chest was rising more than normal, as was my libido.

Brenda feigned being crestfallen.

"She's right. We do need to meet, urgently," I said.

Brenda was disappointed but didn't feel comfortable telling me it could wait. "Okay." She threw her hands in the air. "But I'm not giving up."

"And I won't either. I'll keep at it until she screams out the person's name." I walked Brenda to the door in five short steps. "You can count on me." Gently, I shoved the busybody out the door and shut it in her face as she turned to get in the last word. I placed my ear against the door and, when I heard her retreating footsteps, I locked it as quietly as possible. I turned and noticed Claire trying to look furious at me with her arms crossed, but she was close to laughing.

"So, are we going to do this the hard way?" I demanded.

She cocked her head, not following.

"Stockings. You had to wear stockings today." I smiled.

"What, you don't like the way I look?" I indicated that clearly wasn't the case, and she nodded. "Good. And I'm not getting naked."

"But we have a meeting. A meeting that you requested, I might add." I waggled a finger.

She sashayed over to me, wiggling her hips more than normal, and the effect was working. "I know." Placing her full lips onto mine she kissed me. "Drop them." I felt her fingers tug on my belt, and then she nimbly undid the button and zipper of my trousers. Next she focused on undoing my blouse and unclasping my bra. She sucked on my nipple and then bit it when it became firm in her mouth. Her hand slipped into my panties, and I felt her fingers separate my lips. "Good girl, you're already wet." She thrust her fingers in, and the force of it made me bite down on my lower lip so I wouldn't utter a sound. Claire pushed me against the wall of her office. Her body smashed against me and the wall behind me kept me standing.

With both hands I clutched her tightly against my body. She moved in and out of me with such desire. I thought I would come just from feeling her need to fuck me. I had to be inside her and unzipped her skirt and tugged it down with one swift jerk. Her pantyhose didn't give my hand much room to maneuver, but I wouldn't be stopped. When I slipped inside her, Claire opened her mouth. Quickly, I placed my lips on hers and muffled her excitement. Both of us pumped our hands, and my wrist started to cramp from the angle and pressure. I didn't mind, and it made me quicken my pace. Claire reciprocated. It was like we had a primal need to get the other person to come and to come hard. It didn't feel dirty or cheap. I felt loved completely.

We came, and when the tremors passed we stayed in each other's arms with our fingers inside the other for several moments.

"That was ..." Claire looked into my eyes, and I saw how hers glistened like sapphires.

"Amazing. It was amazing," I whispered. "And I don't want to let go of you."

A ruckus outside brought us to our senses.

"I think the crew's back from lunch," she said into my ear.

I nodded and pulled away to get dressed. "I love you."

She stopped tugging her skirt back up. "That's the first time you've said that to me."

I tucked my shirt into my gray trousers and smiled shyly. "Well, I do love you."

chapter fourteen

I sat at my desk glumly the first Monday morning of July and had zero desire to attend the next strategy meeting. Darrell would more than likely cause a bit of a stink, and I would have to take action. My newspaper sense was going off like a time bomb in my gut.

And then I would have to deal with Claire. A sense of foreboding hung over me like a cloud ready to dump acid rain.

Avery knocked on the door and strutted in before I had a chance to acknowledge her. As usual, her dark hair was pulled back into a tight ponytail, and there were no flyaway hairs.

"I think we should postpone today's meeting," said Avery.

I felt like she'd just tossed me a lifeline after treading in the ocean for hours. "Why?"

"Darrell called. He was in an accident this morning." Avery displayed fake concern on her face, letting me know her true feelings without having to utter them. She was becoming quite cunning, and I admired her way of cementing our bond without risking too much.

"Really?" I cursed the way my voice sounded thrilled with the turn of events. "Is he okay?" I made sure to sound more distressed.

"Yeah, just a minor incident from the sounds of it. But I think it would be nice to—"

"I agree," I cut her off.

Then a thought struck me.

"EXCUSE ME. CAN you tell me where I can find Darrell Miller?" I asked the woman at the front desk. "He was admitted for minor injuries from a car accident." I learned early to give just enough information to seem credible.

"Oh, he's been expecting you. Claire, right?"

I flinched slightly. Claire was picking him up?

"Yes. Claire Nicholls," I said, hoping the woman didn't notice the uncertainty in my body language. I straightened to look more imposing. A tough challenge for someone barely over five feet.

"Here's your ride, Mr. Miller," announced the perky woman as she pulled back the curtain that provided some privacy in the emergency ward.

Darrell locked eyes with me and then smiled at the woman, dismissing her with a curt nod.

When the attendant was gone he demanded, "What are you doing here?"

"I came to see how you're feeling," I responded. I still wasn't positive why I'd come. He never listened to me at the office, so did I really think he would listen to me now? Maybe his brush with death had made him see the light. I imagined the voice of God uttering, "JJ knows what she's doing. Trust her, Darrell Miller."

"Uh-huh. Were you hoping to identify my body?" Darrell forced a sneaker onto his left foot. His neck brace and stiff back limited his mobility.

I helped him with his other shoe. "Can we let bygones be bygones? I want us to work together." My voice was too weak. I was practically begging the man, and that made my stomach churn. Also it gave him the wrong idea.

"And you think showing up here, faking concern, will induce me to play nice in the sandbox?"

I stood up slowly, not wanting to continue the conversation with me at his feet as if pleading for my life. In a way, I felt like I was. Claire had made it clear she didn't want me to fire Darrell. I didn't think it would be a complete deal-breaker, but it would be a difficult hurdle to cross. "Look, you and I want the same thing. We just have different ideas of how to save the paper."

He snorted. The look of triumph in his eyes made me realize how my coming to the hospital looked. I wanted to talk to him outside of work, but it looked too desperate. I bobbed my head, seeing his side. Fuck! This was a huge mistake.

Cora would be so ashamed. I wasn't thinking clearly. I needed to get ahead of the situation and fast. "I didn't have ulterior motives coming here." I was lying, but not for the reason he thought. "I just thought ..." *What did I think?*

Darrell pinned me with a look. "Do you think I was born yesterday, *Ms.* Cavendish?"

I shook my head in frustration. The man didn't want to see what was right in front of him: an olive branch. "Listen—"

He cut me off. "No, you listen. I'm not a newbie. You can't push me around like everyone else. And coming here really shows how desperate you are." Darrell smiled victoriously.

I was desperate but not for the reason Darrell assumed. It was for Claire. "You have no idea—"

He cocked his head. "Don't I? I'm going to be blunt. When I look at you, I see a little girl who's in way over her head. You have no idea what you're doing. You have no idea how to run a paper. My paper!" He thumped his chest. "So don't think showing up here and acting concerned will help your cause. I'm not going to help you. Not one bit." He got in my face.

"Listen, you fool, your paper as you say is about to fail. I'm so tired of dancing around your fucking ego. Personally, I don't give a crap about you. I would have fired you months ago if not …" I had to restrain myself from outing my relationship with Claire.

"Don't threaten me!"

"Threaten you? I'm offering you an olive branch."

He rolled his eyes. "You can't con me. I know what you're up to."

"I'm trying to save your job, you ass."

"Yeah, right." He stood and shoved my shoulder.

I looked at my shoulder and then at him. In a calm voice I said, "If it wasn't for Claire ..." I knew I shouldn't have mentioned her name, but I wanted to get through to him. "We both love her. Can we work together for her sake?" There, I'd stated my true purpose for coming.

"What do you mean, we both love Claire?" He sat down on the exam table. "Are you the one Ian mentioned? The woman who's been spending a lot of time at Claire's house?"

I nodded. "And I know all about Ian."

His face contorted from rage to understanding. But then a look of victory flickered in his eyes.

"You love her that much that you're willing to come here and grovel. I thought you were supposed to be a cold-hearted bitch when it came to business. Beale's Miracle Girl." He crossed his arms. "Don't ever take up the game of poker. You played your cards too soon. I'm going to be brutally honest. I don't like you. I don't like what you're doing to my paper. And I don't want you in Ian's life. Ian has two parents. He doesn't need another."

"Does Claire have a say in this?"

"Claire has always made really poor decisions when it came to relationships."

"You including yourself in that, Darrell?"

He ignored this. "Leave the paper. Go back to New York."

"Or else?"

"Oh, I wouldn't want to ruin the surprise."

I laughed. "Too bad you haven't shown this much initiative in the past eight years. I wouldn't be here right now. You dropped the ball when your wife left and took your kids away. Lost your edge. Your weakness brought me here, and if you think I'm going to back down, you are sorely mistaken."

"What are you going to do? Drag Claire into the middle of all this?" He knew my weak spot because I frigging told him. "Leave Claire out of this."

"I can't. She's what I call my ace in the hole. How will everyone at work treat her if they found out she was fucking the boss? And what if they find out about Ian? Claire has slept with two of the paper's publishers. It's not fair, but you know people will look at Claire differently because she's a woman. They won't treat me any different." He wore a smug smile.

"You're willing to play that card? To humiliate the mother of your son? The paper means that much to you?" What had happened to the man who kept Claire's secret? Who bought his son a Barbie Dream Car? Where was the decent Darrell that Claire kept trying to convince me existed? My body shook with anger.

"How much does it mean to you?" he asked.

I sucked in some air.

"Sorry I'm late, Darrell. Minor emergency at work." Claire barged through the emergency room curtain. "JJ, what are you doing here?" She looked at my flustered face and Darrell's squared shoulders. "What's going on?" Her voice was loud and questioning.

"She's trying to blackmail me," said Darrell.

I backpedaled. "What?" I turned to Claire. "That's not true!" I knew all of us were making a commotion given the setting, but I didn't give a damn. "You fucking bastard!" I started for him, but stopped suddenly.

"Go ahead, JJ. Try me." He didn't mean take a swing at him.

Claire looked to Darrell and then to me.

A nurse barged through the curtain. "What's going on in here? This is a hospital!"

Without responding Darrell pointed at me.

The nurse tapped her foot. "Do I need to call security, Mr. Miller?"

"Yes," responded Darrell gleefully.

"No need, nurse," said Claire. "Really, this is all a big misunderstanding. We'll be out of your hair soon." Claire flashed a scout's honor smile.

The nurse studied Darrell and then my petite frame. "Okay, but if I hear another commotion I'll have security throw all of you out. Understood?"

Claire nodded her head. When the coast was clear, she motioned for Darrell to speak.

"Why else would she be here, Claire?" Darrell turned to me like a cat pouncing on a mouse, except his upper body was stiff as a board, so the move was more Frankenstein-like. "Threatening my job while I'm in the hospital. Low blow, JJ. Low blow." He waggled his finger in disgust. It was clear Darrell planned on using this opportunity to make me look bad, and considering the situation, he was doing a great job. I looked like a schmuck. I'd had no idea that Claire would be the one picking him up, but in hindsight, it made sense for the mother of his son to be listed as an emergency contact.

Claire's chin dropped. The look in her eyes made me want to punch Darrell in the face.

I glared at him. "You know that's not what happened, Darrell. You think you've played your cards well today. Trust me, you fucked up." With that, I spun around and stormed out of the ER, trying not to look defeated and regretting my words. They only made me look guilty. This was why Cora always pounded into me to think with my head, not my heart.

Before escaping into the safety of my car, Claire caught up and tugged my arm. "Would you mind telling me what's going on?"

"I came to offer Darrell an olive branch. He categorically turned me down and declared all-out war." I shook off Claire's hand and disappeared into my car. Without giving Claire a chance to speak, I turned the key and drove off. In the rearview mirror, I saw the puzzled and hurt look on her face grow smaller and smaller until I couldn't see her reflection any longer.

THAT NIGHT, I stood in my apartment, staring at the twinkling lights of Denver, sighing. I was starting to miss New York. The lights. The excitement. It seemed so much simpler back there, and I never thought I'd think that. I had been naïve enough to think conquering the West would be easier for someone from the area.

I wanted a drink, desperately. I rubbed my lips with my palm, trying to erase the need.

Did Claire believe Darrell or me? I was certain he filled her head with lies. In order to combat them, I would have to tell her what he said. Did I want to put a wedge like that between them? How could I tell the woman I loved that the father of her child cared more about the paper than he did about her and their son? After finding me at the hospital, would she even believe me?

And now the writing was on the wall. I had to fire the man. It was obvious he would never give in. Not only did he want the paper back, but he was willing to destroy Claire's career.

Fuck!

I would lose Claire because of him. Because of Darrell *fucking* Miller. The chance for a normal life. A family. I wanted to wring his neck.

The man had nerve when he told the nurse to call security. The thought almost made me smile. He was the one who'd shoved me. I even helped him put his shoe on, for Christ's sake. What an unbelievable ingrate.

"Coming here was a mistake," I muttered before marching over to my fridge in search of a drink. Only bottled water.

Flipping on the TV, I turned to Fox News, not out of support of the channel, but to learn from it. I loved watching how they snared viewers into believing almost anything. Fox personalities were passionate, and I wished I could bottle that passion and slip it into the water cooler at work.

Shit!

I grabbed my car keys and left, returning ten minutes later.

The television was still on, and I tried to watch it and not the whiskey dribbling out of the tiny bottle into a glass filled with Coke. I pondered how long it had been since I had a Jack and Coke, my go-to drink when I needed to let my hair down.

I hoisted the glass to my lips and sniffed the fizzing concoction. The glass was too small to allow for much Coke, and the first sip was mostly whiskey. Closing my eyes, I swished the liquid in my mouth. Fuck, I missed it.

Minutes later, I was concocting another JD, heavier on the whiskey. I had only purchased small bottles of whiskey as a counter-measure. But I did slip the store's card in my pocket. How fortuitous that I found a liquor store in Denver that delivered. So much for Cora implying I was far from civilization. I laughed over the thought of telling her about this latest discovery, but knew she wouldn't find it funny.

Two hours later, a knock on my door startled me.

I peeked through the eyehole and swore under my breath. "Just a minute."

I rushed back into the main room and swept all the tiny whiskey bottles into the trash can next to my desk. Panicking, I crumpled some sheets from my notepad to hide the bottles. Dashing into the bathroom, I quickly gargled some alcohol-free mouthwash.

"JJ, I can hear you in there. Open this—"

Before Claire could utter the word door, I whisked it open and motioned for her to come in.

I looked in the hallway on the off chance that Claire had forced Darrell along for the ride for round two. Not seeing anyone, I shut the door with too much force, which caused me to stagger.

"Can I offer you—" I remembered all the alcohol was gone and stumbled over the words, "a bottled water?"

"This place stinks like a dorm room," was all Claire said. She looked unimpressed by my apartment, which was in complete shambles.

I sniffed my armpit, unsure what Claire meant. Did *I* smell, or the place?

Claire leaned against my desk. "Why did you go to the hospital today?"

"I told you already," I said.

"I asked Darrell about it after you left. He says you threatened his job if he didn't play nice." She crossed her arms and tilted her head.

"Darrell's a goddamn liar," I slurred, and then I quickly covered my mouth in hopes of pushing the garbled words back into my throat.

Claire approached me and sniffed. "Are you drunk?"

Fearful of speaking, I shook my head vehemently.

"I heard clinking before you opened the door," said Claire, not to me but to herself. She spied the trashcan and lifted the crumpled papers. "That's the smell." Her accusatory eyes burned holes into me. "Ten years. You were sober for ten years."

"It's overrated." I waved an arm, accidentally knocking the shade on my librarian desk lamp.

"I can see that. Now you're also looking like an ass, not just acting like one."

"Acting like an ass. You're acting like an ass. You and Darrell." I shook a finger at her. "God, Claire. What did you see in him?" I collapsed into my desk chair.

"I'm wondering the same about you at the moment."

"Pa-lease! Darrell is …" I didn't want to admit what he threatened me with so I uttered, "a country bumpkin. An old fart."

"And you're a snob."

I ignored this comment. "He thinks he has it all figured out. Thinks he can corner me." I waved a hand dismissively. "Darrell has no idea what he's up against."

"So you *did* threaten him today," stated Claire.

"Nope. I tried talking some sense into the man. But he doesn't know his ass from his elbow. I gave him the facts."

She asked, "And the hospital was the best place for this conversation?"

"Obviously not." I shook my head wanly. I wanted to tell her the truth, but didn't think that was the right decision. Exhausted, I slouched in the desk chair. "I went for you, and he saw that I was vulnerable, so he's using it against me. I can't help him now."

"What does that mean?"

"Gone. That's what that means."

"You can't fire Darrell. You promised me."

"I have to. That was the plan. The plan from the beginning." I broke into a fit of giggles. "He was so smug today. Thinking he had me cornered when all along he's been the one stuck in the tree surrounded by wolves." I stopped laughing. "He called me a little girl, today. Said I was a little girl in over my head." I looked for my drink, seeing it was empty. "Damn!" I grabbed my last miniature bottle and poured it into my cup.

"Do you really think you need more?"

"'Do you really think you need more?'" I mimicked. "Yep, I really do."

Claire let out a long breath.

I shrugged and sipped the drink. "Do you have any more accusations to make?" I sputtered.

"You make me sick."

"I make you sick. Interesting coming from the woman who fucked Darrell. Tell me, did he have hair sprouting out of his ears then?"

Claire slapped me across the face before storming out of the apartment.

I shook it off and sipped my whiskey.

THE FOLLOWING MORNING I sat at my desk in the office. It had only been five minutes since I arrived, and I already regretted not staying home. The dawn was still fresh on the horizon, but I wore my sunglasses.

"I hope your head hurts." Claire waltzed into my office.

"Good to see you too, Claire." I removed the glasses gingerly.

"Well?" Claire crossed her arms.

"Well, what?"

"Do you have anything you want to say to me?" Claire's face looked hopeful.

I thought back to last night, remembering snippets. "Not really." What could I say? That Darrell was so determined to get control of the paper that he was willing to throw her and Ian under the bus. It would crush her and threaten Ian's relationship with his father. I couldn't do that.

"That's how it's going to be, then?" asked Claire.

"Yes."

Without saying a word, she left.

My Blackberry rang. Before I had a chance to say hello, Cora shouted, "What in the fuck is going on there?"

"What do you mean?" I popped the top off an aspirin bottle and tossed two pills into my mouth, swallowing without water. Usually I didn't get hungover. Clearly I was out of practice.

"Darrell is telling everyone you went to the hospital to threaten his job. Please tell me you didn't do that." Cora's tone wasn't one of desperation, but animosity.

"Of course not. I went to see if he was okay. I know he's divorced and thought it would be nice to check on him. Not a lot of people are lining up to help Darrell out." How could I tell her I went to ask him to be nice so I wouldn't have to break my promise to Claire? Cora would be appalled by two things. That I asked Darrell for a favor and that I'd made a promise to Claire.

"That's not how it played out."

I wanted to say, "Tell me about it." Instead, I groaned.

"According to my little bird, security threw you out of the hospital." Cora's shrill voice was not helping my throbbing head one bit.

I rubbed my temples. "Another lie. Security wasn't involved. All I did was stop by to see if he was okay. End of story. He's trying to twist it to make me look bad."

"It's working. Get rid of him, now." There was a pregnant pause. "And, JJ, if I hear of you drinking again, I'll fire you myself."

"How did you—?"

Cora cut me off. "How do you think I know? She's concerned about you. Me, at the moment, I'm fucking pissed. Get yourself to a meeting today and every day for the next three months. Am I making myself clear?"

I held onto the phone, listening to the calming effect of the dial tone. I picked up my desk line and called Avery on her cell. "Have the head of HR in my office first thing this morning."

"Righty-O." Kung Fu Avery's voice was too chipper, like she sensed something exciting in the works.

I started to dial Claire's extension, but then thought better of it.

What could I say? I behaved like an ass the night before when she came to talk to me. My ego had taken over. And then there was the whole issue that I was preparing to fire her son's father. I rubbed my forehead in hopes of working the strain out. It didn't. I popped another aspirin into my mouth.

First I had to deal with Darrell. Later Claire.

Julie from HR popped her head around the door promptly at eight. "You wanted to see me?"

I waved the perky blonde woman in. "Yes, and close the door."

Sitting in one of the faux leather chairs opposite my desk, Julie wiped the grin off her face and transformed into a stern professional.

"I need you to put a package together for Darrell. Call Wendell. He knows of the situation and will be able to fill you in on everything."

Julie visibly flinched when I uttered Wendell's name. Wendell was an institution at Beale Media Corp. No other employee caused more fear and dread. If someone was called into his office, it meant he or she was getting fired. No ifs, ands, or buts. Beale Media Corp employees didn't say they were canned. They referred to it as being Wendelled.

Back in the day Wendell would meet with all the employees personally to let them go. Now that most branches had their own HR departments, he was still responsible for doing all the dirty work behind the scenes, but handed off the unpleasant task to the local HR person. It was still called getting Wendelled since everyone knew no one was fired until he got involved.

Julie squirmed in her seat. "A package—you mean he's being let go?"

"Yes. Today. How quickly can you get everything together?"

Julie stood. "Let me get on the horn with Wendell."

"Great. Meet me back here when you're done." Without giving Julie another glance with my bloodshot eyes, I turned my attention to my computer to go over the daily figures. When the door closed, I pulled out a Visine bottle and doused both eyes.

WHEN JULIE REAPPEARED, she was back to her bubbly self. "I think we came up with a decent amount." She handed the paper to me.

I glanced down, nodded in agreement, and then reached for my desk phone. "Avery, please tell Darrell to come to my office."

A moment later Avery called back. "Darrell says he's too busy and asked you to make an appointment for tomorrow."

I saw flashes of red. "Please tell Mr. Miller to come immediately," I instructed Avery.

Julie tittered nervously and mussed with her golden locks. I remembered she was relatively new to the paper and wondered if she'd been involved in firing someone before.

Avery called back. "He's on his way." Her tone suggested I should prepare myself for a charging lion. I felt like a zebra with a broken leg. I steadied my nerves so I could play this just right in front of Julie.

Darrell rushed in. "Who in the fuck do you think you are?" When Julie turned around in the chair with her mouth hanging open, Darrell stopped dead in his tracks.

I motioned for him to have a seat next to the head of HR. "Thanks for making the time, Darrell."

He looked like he was trying to regain his courage, but nodded his head meekly.

"There's never an easy way to do this, so I'm not going to sugarcoat it. While the paper greatly appreciates your dedication and service, we feel it's time for a clean break." I motioned for Julie to hand Darrell his termination notice. "Julie and Wendell have worked out the terms. I hope, given the circumstances, you'll agree it's generous."

Darrell refused to take the paper. Julie wiggled it slightly.

A satisfied smile spread across Darrell's face. "Do you think after yesterday you can do this?"

"What happened yesterday?" I waited to see how he would play this. Would he follow through on his threat? Or did he think I didn't have the balls to call his bluff?

"You. The hospital." Darrell danced around his threat.

"I remember going to the hospital to check on an employee who had been injured in a car accident. Is that what you're referring to?" I kept my face devoid of any emotion.

"You know what I'm talking about." Darrell rubbed the back of his neck, and I realized he wasn't wearing the neck brace he had on yesterday. Stupid macho bullshit.

Julie did her best to sink into her chair, staying out of the fray.

"I'm not sure I'm following. How does yesterday factor into this discussion?"

"You threatened me!" He shouted in triumph, which seemed to cause a twinge of pain, and he grimaced. I hoped it hurt like hell.

I tapped my pen against the side of my computer. "Oh, right." I waved the pen in his direction. "I've heard that rumor. Too bad it's not true, or your lawyer would have a field day."

"Are you calling me a liar?" Darrell still smiled, but it was weakening with each passing second.

"Yes, I am. Do you have any proof of this threat?" I made sure my body language implied I had proof of his.

Darrell remained quiet. His eyes wandered over to the paper resting on the arm of Julie's chair. The moment of truth was almost here. It depended on which one of us would back down, since neither of us was entirely innocent.

I set out my cell phone I normally used to record conversations. I hadn't taped yesterday's confrontation with Darrell, but I hoped the editor wouldn't call my bluff. "I never go anywhere without this. One never knows when you'll need to remember the details. All the details. The sound quality on this gadget is astounding, really. Worth every penny."

Julie let out a small gasp, horrified upon realizing Darrell had lied about everything.

Darrell glared at me. The anticipation was killing me. Would he out my relationship with Claire as well as their past? The seconds ticked by.

Darrell's eyes roved from my phone to the paper.

"Take the deal and I'll forget about everything. Refuse the deal and everyone will hear what's on this." I tapped my phone, leveling my gaze. "I'm assuming you'll be looking for another editing job. There's a job in Cheyenne. I could make a few calls if you'd like."

Darrell slumped into his seat after snatching the paper off Julie's chair.

"Great. Julie will escort you to your office and will help box up your personal belongings. Anything relating to the company, such as your rolodex or whatnot, will stay. Your e-mail has already been shut down." I folded my hands on the desk. "I'm sorry it's worked out this way, but I know you'll land on your feet." I wanted to say *old man*, but thought better of it.

When I was alone, I popped two more aspirin and chased them with cold, bitter coffee. Then I massaged the creases in my forehead, wishing the day was over and not just beginning.

Chiding myself, I buried my attention in reports. The shrill ring of my phone startled me.

"Cheyenne!" Claire's indignant voice was loud enough that I was convinced everyone on all three floors heard.

"Not now. Not here."

"Who do you think you are?"

It was the second time one of my employees had said that to me in the span of three hours.

"Your boss. Do I need to make another call to Cheyenne?" I didn't feel good about the threat. However, Claire needed to learn her place. At least I tried convincing myself.

I could feel Claire's wrath through the phone and then heard a click. Once again, I listened to the dial tone, feeling an odd sense of comfort.

My cell vibrated, and I read Claire's text: *We need to talk.*

This was not the day to have a doozy of a hangover. I didn't respond to the text. I felt the vibration again and read: *Answer me!*

I counted to ten before I calmly texted back that I could meet her at seven that evening. I had five hours before the meeting with Claire. Five hours to pull myself together, get rid of the throbbing headache and the constant urge to heave.

I closed my eyes, remembering my time in the Dominican the previous Thanksgiving. I could hear the lapping waves, feel the warmth of the sun on my skin, and smell the saltwater. I sucked in and slowly let the air seep out, letting go of all the negative feelings.

The phone rang. I ignored it, continuing the exercise my therapist had taught me.

I was back in the lounge chair, listening to a caw of a seagull. A boat on the horizon bobbled on the water.

The phone rang again, and I sensed I had to answer. Avery's voice announced, "Cora's on line one."

I let another deep breath out and then said, "Two times in one day. It's an honor."

"Are you insane?"

"I'm starting to feel that way."

"I saw the package you put together for Darrell. Who do you think you are?"

"No one of importance, apparently."

"Oh, don't play the pity card with me. You're going soft, JJ. And what's this I hear about you finding Darrell another job. What the fuck? We are a media company, not an employment agency. I have my eye on you. Don't ever go behind my back again or Wendell will be calling you! And don't forget about your meeting tonight. I e-mailed you a list of the AA groups in your area."

The dial tone almost sounded like a seagull. I listened intently, but gave up. The daydream was gone.

I WAS NOT in the mood for manners. Instead of knocking on Claire's door, I took the key from the fake rock and let myself in, like I usually did. The shit was about to hit the fan.

Claire was putting dishes away in the kitchen.

"Well, give it to me." I removed my blazer and set it down on the granite countertop.

Claire closed the dishwasher and refused to turn around. "Do you know how far Cheyenne is from here?"

"One hour and forty-four minutes if he takes I-25, according to MapQuest. A little over two hours if he takes highway 85."

Claire flipped around to face me. Tears glistened on her cheeks. "Impressive. What other parlor tricks do you have up your sleeve?"

"I've had a shitty day." I put my hand up to silence the angry woman. "So I'm going to give it to you straight. When I was assigned to this job, I was instructed to fire Darrell when the time was right. I know you can't see it, but he isn't doing the paper any favors. Half of his staff hates him. Finds him dictatorial, bullheaded, and out of touch. The other half is too timid to voice their opinion. We have some great talent. Young talent. George is bursting with ideas, and I know he can turn everything around on his floor. And Darrell has been stifling them for the past couple of years—ever since he lost control of the paper. I don't know if he was doing it intentionally or subconsciously, but he was sabotaging the paper."

I sucked in some air, before continuing. "I had been ordered to give him the boot with very little compensation. I went against Cora and got Darrell the largest package possible, and had my ass chewed out about it by Cora earlier today." I paused to see how Claire took the news, before plunging back into the heart of the matter. "When I found out about Ian, I tried to get Darrell to see the error of his ways, and at the same time I was trying to find him another job in case I couldn't get him on board. No one in Colorado wants to work with him. We work at a paper. There are no secrets in this trade. The only paper I could convince to take him, that was close enough for Darrell to see Ian on the weekends, was Wyoming. It's not part of Beale Media Corp, and the owner is a rich cowboy who has no desire to jump into the twenty-first century. The man uses it for his own political gain, but Darrell won't be forced into using Twitter, Facebook, and all the other things he finds detestable. He'll have to adhere to the guy's political beliefs, but he should be used to that by now. That's just part of the biz."

She remained quiet, and I couldn't gage how she was taking everything.

"Ever since you pleaded with me to protect Darrell I've put my ass on the line more than once. I tried getting him on board. I gave him credit for things he was adamantly opposed to. He couldn't see the writing on the wall." I sighed. "Going to the hospital yesterday was a mistake. I only went to plead with him, for your sake, to ease up a bit."

She watched me wide-eyed. "For my sake?"

"Yes."

"Did you tell him that?"

I was entering the danger zone.

"Did you?"

"Yes."

"So, you've broken two promises to me."

This hurt, but I was also relieved she didn't ask me how Darrell took the news. Claire was the kindest person, but if she found out the threats he'd made in a weak moment, I didn't think she would ever forgive him. And there was Ian to consider.

I wanted to get back on safer ground. "If I let Darrell stay, all of us will be out of a job in five months. I know he's Ian's father, but I can't stand by and let him destroy a paper because he's nursing a wounded ego. Darrell had to go. And then when he started telling everyone at the office I threatened to fire him, when in fact he tried to blackmail me, I was instructed by the CEO of the company to fire him." I cursed myself for saying the word blackmail.

"Blackmail? With what?"

I waved her off. "Nothing for you to worry about," I lied. "We both know Darrell is good at research." I hoped she thought he found out some details about my past. "I believe in this paper, Claire, and I'm not about to walk away."

"Careful, JJ, I can see your ego shining through."

"That may be the case, but at least I know what I'm doing."

"Do you?" Claire cocked her head and raised an eyebrow. "Because after yesterday at the hospital I don't think you do."

I stared at her.

"What about last night?"

"A minor blip … and I know someone has already informed Cora of that blip."

Claire's face flushed.

"Are we done here?" I scooped up my blazer. "I have a meeting to go to."

"Work is never done."

"Not that type of meeting." I turned to go.

"What type of meeting?" Claire's tone softened some.

"Personal and one that Cora insists I go to every day for the next ninety days. Have a good night. We can talk more tomorrow."

"Wait." Claire placed her hand on my shoulder. "I shouldn't have called her. I'm sorry. I was just worried about you."

"I'm curious. Did you ever stop to think that Darrell was lying about yesterday? Or did you automatically assume I was in the wrong because of the poor decisions I've made in the past?"

Claire let her hand fall from my shoulder slowly, like she was unsure if she wanted to break contact but was unable to leave it there.

I waited for Claire to say something. Anything. Or to slap me again. Instead, she walked out of the kitchen and up the stairs to her bedroom, closing the door firmly.

chapter fifteen

"You're quitting?" I was surprised I was able to verbalize the question. Shock. I was in complete and total shock.

"I don't want Ian to grow up without a father."

"And this is the solution? To throw your career away and go to Wyoming?" I waved a hand in the air.

"My career. I'm talking about my son. Besides, I'm not moving to Cheyenne. I'll be staying at my parents' place in Fort Collins. The paper there has been trying to recruit me for years. It's much closer, so Ian can still see his father more than twice a month. Even if Darrell and I met in the middle, it's still two hours Ian has to be in the car. I don't want my child to feel like luggage always being handed off. Besides, with our jobs, it'll be impossible for both of us to leave the office on schedule every time." Claire avoided looking at me while she spoke.

"I know you're pissed at me for firing Darrell, but stop and think what you are doing. Don't react. Think." I placed my hands on her shoulders.

"Ha! Should I learn from your example?"

"What does that mean?"

"That night. That night you left me."

"I left you?" I staggered back. "If I recall, you left me. But not before you told me you were planning to marry Andrew. And I was only going away for six months."

"Six months? You didn't come back for over twenty years!" She threw her arms up and let out an angry rush of air.

"Come back for what? You were planning on marrying Andrew." My voice cracked as the anger flowed through each letter.

She waved it all away. "I never married Andrew!"

"But you planned to. It's not like you sent me a letter or anything saying you called off the wedding and why."

She sat down heavily on the side of my desk. "Andrew called it off."

I collapsed into my chair. "What?"

"Andrew called off the wedding."

"I know—"

Claire cut me off. "He called it off because he knew I didn't love him and that I loved you. He told me to find you and to tell you."

"Why—?"

Again she cut me off. "I wanted to. I tried to. I called your parents and asked when your flight was supposed to arrive. I planned on meeting you at the airport …"

I covered my face with both hands and spoke. "But I didn't come home. I went to New York at the last second."

I still hid my eyes with my hands, but I knew she was nodding her head solemnly.

"Fuck!" I slammed a fist down on my desk.

She sighed, and I could tell Claire was trying to hold back a sob. "Do you ever think that we were never meant to be? That all the signs are telling us to stop."

I looked her in the eyes. "No. I don't think that, and I never did."

"I love you, but I have to think of my son. He adores his father. I know Cheyenne isn't that far away, but for a child it's as far as the moon. Besides, you keep warning me that the doors here may close come the new year. *Fort Collins Gazette* called me two days ago with the offer. I was going to turn it down, but now, I think it was a sign. It's the third time they've offered me the position. You know what they say about the third time being the charm." She started to laugh, but it died abruptly.

"What about us? How we talked about adopting? I make plenty. You could stay home. Like you always wanted."

"And if *Mile High* closes?"

"Claire, I won't be out of a job. I could be CEO of this company someday."

"And then Ian would be in New York and would only see his father during the summer and on holidays."

I bit my lower lip so I wouldn't swear. "We could work it out. Maybe I could get Darrell a job in New York. They'll be more opportunities."

"JJ …"

"Is it because of the other night? It was just a blip. I plan on going to meetings. I'll go every day of my life if you ask. All you have to do is ask. I'll do anything for you."

"It's not just the other night. So much has happened over the years. Me with Ian. You and … There's so much water under the bridge, and I'm not sure we can get past that."

Claire looked away, and I could tell her mind was made up. I sat in my chair, dumbstruck.

Claire then held my gaze for several seconds. "I'll have my official letter of resignation on your desk first thing tomorrow morning. It's easier this way. Safer for Ian and me."

With that, she left my office.

I covered my mouth with a shaky hand, fearful what I might say or do. The clock on the wall behind me ticked loudly, and each passing second felt like a lifetime.

Safer?

Did she mean safer not to settle down with a former addict?

Reaching for the phone, I hit the first number on my speed dial.

"Hello?" Her voice was perky for someone who was usually dictatorial.

"I need—" A sob rendered me speechless.

I heard Cora on the other line, breathing. I held the phone with one hand and rubbed my forehead with the other.

Finally, she spoke. "What do you need, JJ? Tell me and I'll do it."

I sucked as much air as possible into my lungs so I could get the statement out. "Get me out of this fucking state before—" I couldn't complete my thought since I didn't know what I was capable of at the moment.

"Listen to me. I'm getting on the next flight to Denver. Promise me that you won't do anything stupid."

"Define stupid."

"Go to your apartment and wait for me. Don't go to work tomorrow. I'll call Avery and take care of everything. Promise me you won't do anything. Don't drink. Don't run away. Don't disappear. Whatever pops into your fucking shit for brains, just don't do it. Stay put."

I remained mute and considered all the possibilities she had just provided. I could get into my car and start driving. I had enough money in my accounts to survive for a few years. Even more if I cashed in my 401(k). Alaska. The thought of endless Alaska brought a smile to my lips. No one would look for me in fucking Alaska! Who in their right mind would run away to Alaska?

"JJ!" The sharpness and desperation in Cora's tone brought me back.

"Yes."

"Yes, what?"

"I promise, Cora. I promise."

"Before I go, can you tell me one thing?"

I nodded, knowing she would pick up on it somehow. She always did.

"Is it Claire?"

"Y-yes." I forced back the tears by rubbing my eyes so hard I thought they would pop out.

"I'm sorry, sweetie. I'm on my way. Go home and get some rest if you can."

Again I nodded my head numbly. I heard the click of the phone and knew Cora was going into action mode. Before heading to the airport she'd call Avery and take care of everything. Cora was excellent at taking care of things.

I was excellent at destroying things these days. Every addict needed a friend like Cora to help pick up the pieces. I imagined my life was like a game of Jenga: always teetering to one side, ready to crash down. I told my therapist this once, and she replied, "That's your problem. You treat life like a game. Why do you think you do that?"

I hated that she always ended each response with a question. I answered, "How should I treat it?"

"One day at a time."

I laughed in her face. The addict's motto drove me absolutely insane. One fucking day at a time. Okay, one day at a time I took another piece out of my life, causing it to teeter precariously a little bit more each day. One day at a time. Until it all fell down and I was left with nothing.

CORA RAPPED ON my door five minutes after midnight. She must have dashed to the airport right after we got off the phone.

She set her emergency overnight bag that she kept at the office down in the entryway like a woman unburdening herself from all her worries. She then wrapped her arms around me. "I flew coach just for you."

I melted into her arms even more, knowing that even though she was a hard-ass ninety percent of the time, she really was my closest and most supportive friend.

"Is this the moment when I say 'It's okay. Just take it one day at a time?' I know how much you love that piece of advice." She rubbed my back.

"Only if you want to turn around and take the next flight out of here," I mumbled into her shoulder.

"Can I at least shower first? I always feel like I need to take five showers to get the filth of coach off me." She stepped back to eye me.

"Must be hard being among the masses after all those years in your ivory tower."

"Says the woman who runs one of the largest papers in Colorado." She lifted my chin with her slender finger. "Put some coffee on. I'll be out of the shower in a jiffy. Then you and I are going to talk until the sun comes up."

I did as instructed. Cora wasn't kidding. Before I had a chance to pour a cup she was standing in the kitchen in my bathrobe, towel drying her hair. "It's been a long time since I stayed the night at your place." She winked at me suggestively. "Of course back then, I needed to shower for different reasons."

I poured a cup for her. "Does your husband know about us?"

She crinkled her brow. "Of course. Why?"

"Just curious, I guess. It doesn't worry him that you're here with me?"

"Not in the least." She poured some milk into her coffee. "He asked me once why we didn't work out."

I raised my cup to my lips and then said over the brim, "What did you say?"

"Your heart belonged to another. It always had."

This was never stated while we were an item, but when she called it off, she told me that was the way I made her feel. I never denied it.

"I'm sorry."

She waved me away. "Don't be. It was fun while it lasted." Her smile reminded me of why I'd bedded her in the first place. Cora was captivating: beautiful, intelligent, witty, powerful, and damn right sexy. Many people would give anything to be with her. But she wasn't Claire.

Cora beckoned me to the front room by wiggling her finger. She sat on the couch, and I sank into one of the chairs. "Now tell me. What happened? Last time I was here you were head over heels in love."

I sipped my coffee. "Where do I begin?"

"The beginning, of course, you numbskull."

So I did. I started from the day I met Claire. I had never told Cora much about my past. I never spoke about Claire to anyone really. Some of my exes, like Cora, guessed there was someone who broke my heart, but when pushed to share, I never would.

Cora sighed when she heard about Darrell being Ian's father. "Oh, JJ. Why didn't you tell me?"

"Would it have changed your mind?"

Cora smiled guiltily. "No, but we could have talked about it. Tried to think of something."

"I thought I *had* thought of something. Cheyenne isn't that far away from here." I rested my head on the back of the chair. "I had no idea Claire would quit her job and move to Fort Collins to be closer to Darrell *fucking* Miller."

Cora put a hand up. "Are you going to tell her about his threat?"

I shrugged. "Not sure I should. Yeah, it might repair some of the damage between us, but what about Ian? You're a mother. How would you react?"

She bit her lower lip and bobbed her head. That was answer enough.

"So, you'll be a secret martyr. I admire that. But what will it do to you in the long run?"

"Have you ever thought I'm broken beyond repair? This whole Miracle Girl and shit. It's always hanging over my head." I looked her in the eyes. "And don't blame yourself for it. I dug my own grave."

She let out a snort of laughter. "You're always so concerned about those around you. You need to start taking care of yourself."

"I can't tell her. It'll crush her. Besides, Darrell backed down from his threat, and I blackmailed him in front of Julie. I'm not innocent in this whole situation. It's messy. And trying to explain it will only muddle the waters."

Cora pinned me with an inquisitive look. "You really do love her. I mean, *really* love her."

"Yes. From that first moment."

She laughed good-naturedly. "Oh my tough little JJ is a walking cliché."

I frowned.

"Do you think, with time, the damage can be repaired?" she asked.

"Maybe. But how much time? Last time it was twenty-five years."

"What's your next step?" Her eyes grew big with anticipation.

"I want out. Get me the fuck out of Colorado. Please. I want to come home." I didn't even have the decency to cringe over the groveling in my voice.

Cora collapsed back onto the couch, disappointed yet again. "You're always leaving. Twenty-five years ago you did, and you've been doing it ever since. As your friend, I won't let you. And as your boss, I'm ordering you to stay."

"I'm not sure I can. I'm suffocating, and I'm scared."

"I know, sweetheart. But you'll feel that way wherever I send you, and I need you here."

"And how do you propose I survive here."

Cora flashed me a wicked smile. "Why, one day at a time of course." Her malicious grin managed to still seem somewhat heartfelt. "And keep going to meetings regularly again. You need to find a release so you can think clearly. Open up there. Let them help you heal. I think you may find you aren't alone."

I ignored this bit. "How did you know about Darrell's threat, anyway?

Does Avery ever sleep, or is she always following me around to keep tabs on me?"

"Avery isn't my spy. At least knowingly. She's probably the only person at the paper you can trust."

"Tell me, wicked one, how do you keep your fingers in so many pots?"

"Ha! A true sorceress never reveals her powers." She closed her eyes, exhausted from having stayed up all night. "Let's take a nap and then have some breakfast before I head back."

The thought of her leaving so soon terrified me, but I knew she couldn't stay. The fact that she'd dropped everything for me was enough to keep me going for the next few days.

chapter sixteen

Brenda's office looked worse than if a tornado had ripped through it. The stack of papers, coffee-stained mugs, dirty dishes, random clothes, and what looked to be a cat water bowl and food dish (with bits of kibble strewn about) didn't impress me much. I wouldn't be surprised if I discovered a toilet seat and a beat-up washing machine from the 1950s in there. Her office was twice the size of Claire's, but it was in the back of the building, under the stairwell. At one point, it must have been a storage place, and I wasn't at all surprised that was where the office kook was tucked away.

"Have a seat, JJ." Brenda motioned to the one chair that had a stack of files on it.

"That's fine. I've been sitting all day," I tried to explain away my rudeness. There was no way I was stepping one foot into her domain. I leaned against the doorjamb with my arms crossed. "How's the planning going?"

Brenda nearly jumped out of her skin when I asked for a volunteer to put together Claire's going away party. She had put her notice in three weeks ago. At the end of the week, Claire would no longer be an employee of *Mile High*. At the office, we maintained a professional relationship. After hours, Claire was doing everything in her power to avoid me. I was starting to wonder if she had changed her phone number.

Usually I didn't get involved with the planning of these types of affairs, but I felt compelled to follow up with Brenda. And by the looks of the circulation director's office, I was a bit worried that she'd forgotten about it completely.

"I was able to book the Olive Garden for Saturday." Brenda had a red pen tucked behind an ear and another dangling on her necklace.

"That's great. And the cake?"

I offered to pay for the cake and asked Brenda to order one from the local shop that was featured on some food channel. The owner constructed elaborate cakes that resembled anything the client wanted.

"Yep. At first I asked if they could make a cake that was a mini-Ian."

I held my breath.

"But then they said Claire may not like people carving into her son." She laughed over the prospect. "I guess I see their point."

I smiled tentatively, unsure if I wanted to probe further into what she'd actually designed. This was the first and last party I was letting Brenda plan.

"But we came up with something I think she'll love. Of course I would prefer if she didn't leave. I'm not sure I'll know what to do once she's gone." She looked how I felt on the inside.

"I'll double your salary and give you two months paid vacation if you can talk her into staying." The words slipped out, and I tried covering up my blunder with a forced laugh. I wasn't lying.

Brenda looked at me, unclear if I was serious or not. "I know, right?" She went the safe route.

"I … the paper needs her. We all need her. Well, thanks for taking care of everything." I looked at my watch. "I have to run."

Brenda mumbled bye. As I looked over my shoulder before leaving her department, I saw her peeking her head out the door, looking more befuddled than ever. I gave a half wave, and she returned it with a lackluster dip of her head.

WHEN I WALKED into the restaurant, it looked as though every staff member had shown up for Claire's send-off. I had been to several going away parties, but this was the first with such a turnout. Everyone loved Claire. Respected her. And no one wanted to see her leave.

Quickly, I glanced around and didn't see Darrell. I was about eighty percent positive he'd be a no-show, considering Claire was bringing Ian. They had kept the secret for so long I couldn't imagine them spilling it now. Claire was a creature of habit.

Ian stood next to his mother, looking overwhelmed. When I approached he smiled at me, relieved to see a friendly face. He motioned with his hand that he wanted to share a secret. I kneeled down, and he whispered in my ear, "Do you think there are any rabbit turds in the cake?" Then he started laughing.

Placing a hand on his shoulder, I whispered back, "I ordered them just for you." I handed him a wrapped gift. "I got you this."

Ian's eyes grew large, and he looked up at his mom, imploring her with a smile to let him open the gift. She nodded. He ripped the paper off in less than a second. "Cool!"

Claire looked at the Xbox Just Dance game I got her son. She did her best to repress a smirk, but I saw a trace of a smile pull at her lips. "What do you say, Ian?"

"Thanks, JJ. I love to dance." He gripped the game with both arms and twirled around.

"I know, buddy. And you'll be the best dancer in Fort Collins."

I stood up and saw Brenda eying me intensely. She grabbed my arm and then said conspiratorially, "I need to borrow JJ for a moment." She pulled me into the back room. I expected her to ask what the deal was about buying Ian a gift, but instead she said, "Here it is!" She mimicked a drum roll and then waved her arm to the cake.

It was a massive newspaper spread open. The black and white icing turned my stomach. Not because of the colors, but because it was a symbol of Claire leaving to work at another paper. Leaving me. For once it was someone in my life leaving and not me.

I swallowed hard. "Oh, this is great. Really, really great." I circled the cake, feigning admiration instead of stomping it to bits like I wanted.

"So …" Brenda looked past my shoulder to make sure the coast was clear. "Do you think this has anything to do with Claire's mystery beau?"

My head snapped up too quickly, leaving me exposed.

She didn't notice.

"I think Claire's in love with a younger man." She paused. "Or woman." She winked at me, her lesbian boss. "And she's afraid to spill the beans. She's being cagey about why she finally accepted the job up there, and she's never cagey with me. It has to be something big."

I felt weak in the knees, but did my best not to show it. "You know, I bet you're right." With that, we rejoined the party.

After some time, it was clear Claire felt overwhelmed, and I saw her slip outside for a cigarette. We hadn't spoken privately since she turned in her resignation. I decided this was my final chance.

"I'm sorry I didn't get you a gift," I said as I approached with my pack of cigarettes out for her to take one.

She grabbed one, and I had my lighter ready. Claire inhaled deeply. Raising the cigarette in front of her face, she mumbled, "Thanks."

I couldn't think of anything to say that would whisk her off her feet, so I stayed quiet.

"It was sweet of you to get Ian a gift." She looked nervous to be alone with me. "His father will love it."

I smiled. "Yes, but that's not the reason I got it."

She studied me and then let it go.

"How is Darrell?" I asked as I stared at the stars, remembering her comment that for a child Cheyenne was as far away as the moon. I wished I was on the moon, far away from all this pain and loneliness.

"Good. He's getting settled in."

I nodded. "That's great. I hope—"

"You and Brenda are becoming fast buds." She nudged my shoulder playfully.

"Yeah, I think she thinks we'll be bfs now that you're leaving."

"You couldn't ask for a better friend at the paper. You'll learn that." She was actually being sincere, so I decided not to say how I really felt.

"I'll take care of her." I puffed on my cigarette before I said the dreaded words *I promise.*

Claire squeezed my arm.

"So, are you all packed?"

"We don't have to bring much. My parents' place is furnished, and Ian is excited to live in a cabin. He's been reading books about Davey Crockett."

This made both of us laugh.

"You nervous about your job?" I asked.

She shrugged. "A little. Hadn't had much time to think about it though."

"If you ever need to talk, I'm just a phone call away."

She tamped out her cigarette in an ashtray. "I better get back inside."

"Claire, wait." She turned and faced me. "If you need anything …"

Tears formed in her eyes. "Same with you."

We stood, not speaking. Finally, she said, "You coming in?"

"In a moment. I miss seeing the stars." I waved pathetically at the sky.

Moments later, I felt someone slip their arm through mine. I thought it was Claire and rested my head on the person's shoulder.

"I'll miss her, too," said Brenda, and she patted my arm.

I didn't pull away. "There's no one else like her in this world."

Brenda's silence surprised me.

chapter seventeen

First thing the following Monday morning, I headed to the dreaded meeting with all the department heads. I had decided late last night, after smoking a pack of cigarettes on my balcony until two in the morning, that it was time for them to know the whole truth.

I sat in my chair at the head of the table and waited for Brenda to take her seat. No one was missing, besides Claire and Darrell. Out of the remaining nine, no one looked eager to be there.

Clearing my throat, I began in a quiet voice. "I know many of you are scared about the recent changes. All of you have integrity, and many of you are hesitant about all the modifications I have been imposing. Some of you probably think I'm degrading the paper. I get that. I do."

I looked around the table. Every eye was on me. "But I'm not in a position to create a paper that would make my folks proud. There aren't many like my folks anymore who want real journalism.

"The fact of the matter is most people don't crave news anymore. Scandal, sex, gossip … that's what is trending on Twitter. That's what they crave."

Standing, I continued to talk while I walked the circumference of the room. "Attention spans are rapidly shrinking. Texting and Twitter are killing the English language. LOL, hashtags, smiley faces—that's how people communicate these days. I'm not saying we should publish trash. We have to find a balance."

I leaned against the far table so I could see everyone. "Going back to my earlier point, I would love to create a paper that would make my parents proud. I know we all would. I would love for our writers to win awards and to bring honor to this paper.

"But right now, I have to face the facts. And I've held back on some crucial points to protect all of you." I crossed my arms.

"I think that was a mistake, and I'm sorry. Here's the truth. If our numbers don't drastically improve by December thirty-first, corporate is shutting us down."

The murmuring started, like I knew it would. I gestured with my hand for quiet. "I understand that's not what any of you want to hear, but you need to hear it. It's almost August. We have less than half a year to succeed.

"I am willing to do everything in my power to make sure we do. Even if I have to sell my soul to the fucking devil, I want to keep our doors open. Come January first, I want all of you to have jobs."

I looked everyone in the eye as I waited for a brief moment to let that bit sink in. "So I'm asking all of you to pitch in and help. I mean, really pitch in."

I slapped the tabletop with my palm. "And fucking stop fighting with me. I'll make you this promise. Once we get back on our feet, we can work on rebuilding our integrity. But now isn't the time to act high and mighty. Now's the time to get our hands dirty. If you can't do that, I ask that you leave this room now."

Several people looked around the room to see if anyone would leave. No one did.

"Good. Let's work together. Come back tomorrow morning prepared with ideas."

People started to leave, muttering to whoever was exiting with them. Hopefully that would light a spark under their asses.

Brenda stayed behind. When it was just Avery and me, she clapped her hands. "Bravo, JJ. I was starting to wonder if you had it in you." She nodded her head approvingly and left the room.

Avery turned to me with eyebrows raised. "I can't figure her out."

"I think I'm starting to."

chapter eighteen

The weeks following Claire's leaving stacked up quickly. I buried myself in work, and when I wasn't working I went for long runs or bike rides. Cora was trying to convince me to train for a triathlon. And when I wasn't exercising, I attended AA meetings. Things were finally looking up at work. My come-to-Jesus talk scared the bejeezus out of most of the staff, and many rolled up their sleeves and got to work. One department head refused to play nice, so I fired him. That terrified the rest to try even harder.

Claire and I exchanged e-mails and some texts, but it was clear to both of us that it was painful. Neither one of us, though, had the balls to say it, so we both kept up the image that we could be friends.

Before I knew it, three months had gone by.

I stood in front of the group. It had been years since I'd done this, and I foolishly thought I was in the clear. That I'd kicked booze and drugs for good. But as cliché as it sounded, addicts really did have to take it one day at a time. Fucking hell, I hated admitting that.

"I had been sober for ten years. Actually, I had stopped counting the days around the seventh year." I gripped the podium. "Three months ago I took a drink. Then another and another. You see, there was this woman I loved when I was just a kid, and then we reconnected recently. I finally thought I could have everything I always wanted, but never knew it until it was within my grasp. A partner. A family … but life has a way of putting up roadblocks." I paused and many in the group murmured in understanding. I continued speaking, laying out my sob story and finished with, "Ninety. I'm ninety days sober once again." There was applause, but it felt hollow without Claire.

After the meeting, I wanted to hightail it out of the room, not stop for idle you-can-do-it chitchat. I was ashamed. Cora hadn't given me an option. If I wanted to keep my job, she'd overlook my transgression as long as I took the necessary steps to stay sober. And with the whole Claire fiasco she knew I needed support more than ever. That meant attending AA meetings. After the first month I argued with her on the phone. How would I find the time to go to meetings every day?

Her response was pretty typical. "You used to find the time for coke and drinking. I'm sure it won't be that difficult to squeeze in, really."

I hated when people said this shit. It made it crystal clear how fucked up I'd let my life get back then and how hard I had to fight today to stay clean.

"Excuse me," said a woman in her late twenties.

"Yes," I replied, still itching to get the hell out of the church basement before others had time to approach me and hand me their numbers saying, "If you need to talk, call me."

The brunette, who was attractive in the girl-next-door way, blushed. "I'm sorry, I'm kinda new to this. I just wanted to say I was touched by you tonight." She turned redder, and I felt like I could feel the heat radiating from her face. "I don't mean literally of course, but by your words. Gosh, maybe I should stop now before I make a bigger ass out of myself." She put her hand out. "My name is Janie."

Janie's hand was clammy, and I remembered what it was like when I first started AA. Her innocent milk-chocolate eyes implored me to be kind. There was a flicker of something else in her eyes, but I pushed that aside. Getting involved with someone from AA was not recommended.

"Would you like to grab a cup of coffee or something?" I asked, kicking myself for doing so.

She shuffled her feet nervously, and I could see her mulling over the idea. "Y-yeah, that would be nice."

By the second cup of coffee in the shop around the corner from my apartment, I knew I was in trouble. There was this intensity every time our eyes locked. Once, we both reached for the sugar and our fingers touched. There was a jolt of desire, and it whizzed around my body before it settled in my nether regions, causing my pussy to throb with desire. *I don't need this*, I told myself. *This would be a horrible mistake. Nothing good would come from this. Just stop, JJ. Think of the consequences. Think of Claire. Having a fling with someone in her twenties isn't going to help you win Claire back. Sure, she insinuated she wasn't sure about being with an addict, but staying clean might convince her otherwise.*

The debate in my head continued. *She's much younger than you. She didn't come to AA to hook up with anyone. Don't do this.*

"Would you like to come over to my place?" I asked, ignoring common sense and decency.

A slight smile of recognition inched across Janie's face, and her eyes glowed with the feeling that the night was just beginning. "That would be nice."

I didn't waste any time whisking her outside. I feared my brain would interfere with my desire if given half the chance to think. If I couldn't have a drink to get my mind off Claire, I would need another form of release. Hadn't Cora said I needed to find a release for my pent-up emotions? And Janie provided the perfect opportunity. This made me feel slimy, but it didn't stop me.

A FEW WEEKS later, I waltzed out of my office, ushering one of our citizen bloggers out. "Thanks so much for coming in today." The woman blushed again. She had kept blushing from the moment we met. Her blog post had gone viral last week. It was about how the press treated the indiscretions of female movie stars, which showed that the double standard from the fifties was alive and well. Avery suggested I bring her in to say congratulations, take some photos, and start a new competition among our bloggers. Unfortunately, due to my schedule, the timing of the meeting was off. I was in a rush to grab a coffee and smoke before dashing off to a charity event hosted by several prominent wives. I'd rather have my left foot run over repeatedly with a lawn mower, but this was all part of the job. At least it wasn't a black tie event and I could show up in a suit.

"If you need anything, just let Avery or me know. You're our star blogger. Keep up the excellent work." I continued to smile as I walked her to the elevator.

There was a commotion at Avery's desk, but I positioned my body so the woman couldn't see what was happening. Once the elevator closed, I walked to Avery's desk to find Janie arguing with my assistant.

What was going on? I glanced at my watch, sighing.

"Hey you, what are you doing here?" I placed a kiss on Janie's cheek. Avery had patched a few of Janie's calls through, so I made no attempt to hide the fact that I was seeing her. Cora had told me to trust Avery, so I did.

"I thought I'd pop in and see if you were available for dinner," she explained, all the while staring at Avery like she wanted to rip her toenails off. We had been seeing each other for a few weeks, and I had never invited her to my office.

Avery wore her confident smile that could mean any number of things, but I suspected she wasn't too thrilled with my current fling. It wasn't that Janie was a woman. Everyone knew that about me. But Janie was so much younger than me, closer to Avery's age, and impertinent enough to pop in unannounced. Since Darrell and Claire's departure, my schedule didn't allow time to breathe, let alone to participate in idle chitchat.

"Actually, I'm on my way out to a charity event. Would you like to grab a cup of coffee with me?"

"That'd be great." Janie looked at Avery with a grin that suggested she wanted to say, 'I told you so.'

"Before you go, Ms. Cavendish, I need you to sign some papers." Avery tapped her pen against her thigh.

"Of course." I suppressed a smile and thought it clever of her to call me Ms. Cavendish as a way to inform Janie that this was a professional setting, not junior high. But I wasn't entirely sure who she was admonishing.

I told Janie I would meet her at the elevator in a jiff.

As soon as she was out of earshot, I asked Avery what papers I needed to sign.

She ignored me. "I've seen her before, but I can't remember from where. I have a bad feeling, JJ. A very bad feeling."

This rattled me some, and I pictured Avery's Krav Maga instincts going into hyper drive, but I pushed the notion out of my head. "The papers,

Avery."

"Oh. Here they are."

I signed them and rushed off.

When the elevator doors closed, Janie kissed me forcefully. I felt like she was staking her claim and wondered if she suspected that I was also seeing Avery.

"So, do I need to schedule our meetings through Avery from now on?" she said as she ran her finger down the front of my blouse.

That made me laugh. "Oh, I would love to hear that during my morning briefings. 'You have lunch with the mayor, a three o'clock staff meeting, and a fuckfest with Janie at nine.'"

This appeased her some, and she kissed me again quickly before the doors opened.

The coffee shop was just down the street, and within minutes we both had a latte in one hand and a lit cigarette in the other. We sat on the edge of a small pond and took in its rock formation with a fierce looking eagle on top. Upon further scrutiny, I saw that a snake dangled from the eagle's mouth. Water gushed down the rocks, and I could feel a slight spray on my hand.

Janie followed my eyes. "Are you a fan of Western art?"

"It's funny. I never thought I was, but being back here, I'm realizing how much I missed it." I sipped my coffee. "Sometimes I feel like the snake." I motioned to the eagle's mouth.

"No wonder, with people like Avery on your staff." She looked away.

"Oh, it's not Avery I'm worried about."

Janie's head snapped back to me, and for a brief moment she looked like I had just stuck a gun in her back. The muscles in her face relaxed as quickly, and she leaned close to me and said, "Who are you afraid of?"

I laughed. "Oh, the list is far too long to get into now." I glanced at my watch. "What are you doing later tonight?"

"Hopefully fucking your brains out," she said without any indication that I would be offended by her words.

I wasn't. Janie was a wonderful distraction.

"Good. My place or yours?"

"Yours of course." I still hadn't been to her place. I assumed she was embarrassed by her accommodations. I imagined being a hostess at a steak joint didn't pay all that much. However, whenever I offered to go to her place, she found an excuse to meet at mine instead.

"Meet me there around ten."

She nodded.

I stood in front of her awkwardly, not knowing what to do. "Okay, then. See you later." I kissed the top of her head and left without either of us saying another word. Guilt inched up slowly like a spider crawling up the length of my body. Shaking off the creepy tingling sensation, I headed for the event. Soon, I would be in bed, naked with Janie, forgetting everything.

chapter nineteen

"I'm not sure we want to go that route," said Brenda.

Avery countered, but I didn't have the heart to listen to their debate. Brenda was the most experienced director left at the paper, and once a week the three of us met to discuss the paper's next move in a more private setting. The Monday morning meetings continued with all the directors of course. However, these smaller meetings were more fruitful.

One of the last things Claire said to me was I should put my faith in Brenda. Cora told me that Avery was trustworthy, so I let her in more. I realized I couldn't save the paper on my own. Every time we made some inroads, we started hemorrhaging in a different area. We'd increase online subscribers, yet some of traditional advertisers balked and left. Or we'd have a successful blog competition only to annoy some of the writers on our staff. It was an endless battle. I was starting to think no matter how hard we fought, we would lose the war. We needed a fucking Hail Mary. Like the time I met Cora in a coffee shop three days after I arrived in New York, jobless after my backpacking trip. We talked about my travels, and Cora offered me a job as a travel writer on the spot.

I studied Brenda's outfit and hair. She looked more like a bag lady on the streets, the way her striped bulky sweater hung off her even though she wasn't a skinny woman. Underneath she wore a plaid shirt, and her ginger corduroy pants didn't match either her shirt or sweater. Her hair, as usual, was completely out of control. Yet when she spoke about important matters she was confident, intelligent, and insightful.

Avery was the exact opposite. My assistant always looked put together, and I suspected her clothes were even more expensive than mine. Her hair and makeup were flawless. Avery exuded confidence. Brenda looked like a clown. Yet, both were great at their jobs and complemented each other well.

Avery got up to leave, but Brenda stayed put. As soon as Avery was out of earshot, Brenda said, “So that day in Claire’s office, both of you played me for a fool.” Her tone suggested she wasn’t bitter, but finally in on the joke.

Only I didn’t know what joke she was talking about. “I’m sorry. What?”

“Oh come now. When I was trying to determine who Claire was seeing, it was you, wasn’t it?” Brenda jutted her chin out and furrowed her brows.

Hesitating momentarily to determine if Claire had said anything, I realized Brenda was fishing.

I shook my head. “Sorry. Not it.”

At the moment I wasn’t involved with Claire, and I hoped that helped me appear sincere.

Brenda examined my face like she was waiting for some sign that I was fibbing. “Nope. It’s you. Or it was you.” She looked away, not expecting me to answer or to lie again. “Ever since you came to my office about Claire’s going away party, I knew I was missing something. The other day I had lunch with Claire and mentioned how you joked that you would give me a raise if I could convince you to stay. The look on her face told me everything. I started to suspect when she pulled me aside on her last day and asked me to help you. Claire was never one to ask for favors, and I knew there had to be a good reason. I mulled it over, and the only thing that makes sense is love.”

“Love?”

“Jesus, JJ. For someone who’s supposed to be brilliant you really are nutty.” Brenda sipped her coffee that surely was cold by now.

It was hard not to burst into a gale of laughter. Brenda the mad woman was calling me nutty. She was the nutter.

Brenda ignored me completely and continued talking, more to herself.

"To think, wrecking a relationship with Claire. Beautiful, honorable, caring—you couldn't find a better person, and to muck it up. For what?"

She leveled her gaze on me, including me in the conversation once again.

"The job. I bet you did it for the job." She blew out some air, disturbing the hair that hung in front of her left eye.

The nutter looked away from me and continued debating on her own. "But what about the job. What set Claire off? It couldn't have been Darrell. Everyone knew he'd be the first to go."

I shifted in my chair, uncomfortable.

Brenda raised an eyebrow. "It was Darrell, wasn't it? There was a time when they were super-close, but then something happened. Claire took some time off to have Ian, and when she returned, she barely said two words to Darrell. I asked her about it, but she just said that she was a single mother and was too busy to talk to anyone."

I noticed that she had stopped talking, and I looked back in her direction. There was a look of clarity on her face.

I was tiring of this interrogation, or whatever it was. But I was also intrigued. This woman was a lot more perceptive than I gave her credit for. Actually, I hadn't given her any credit before.

"I hope it's worth it."

"What?" I forced the word out and cringed to hear my voice crack like a teenager caught sneaking into the house after curfew.

"Whatever you chose over Claire."

Ironically, I did choose Claire. To protect her at least.

In the past I had been lectured by many and told by a few that I'd let them down. It was never a pleasant experience, but I was pretty quick to shake it off. But the rebuff by Brenda, for some reason, stung the most. Maybe because she actually verbalized what I had been feeling ever since Claire left. I had the perfect woman and lost her. Again. Brenda didn't know the true reason why Claire left. No one but Cora and Claire knew my history. My past. If only I could shed my past.

When Brenda left, I reached for my phone. Letting out a sigh, I dialed Janie's number. Her energetic hello didn't cheer me up. "I feel like leaving the office early today. You want to meet me at my place in an hour?"

chapter twenty

I sat by the window in my bedroom, smoking a cigarette. I had popped the screen out so I could ash outside. The heat was cranked so I could leave the window open. It was only November, but winter had decided to arrive early. My thick terrycloth bathrobe was tied tightly around me. Janie lay in bed, naked. We'd just had a marathon love making session. A blanket draped over her midsection exposed her tiny breasts and slender left leg.

I knew my relationship with Janie couldn't last much longer. She was exciting and all, but I didn't just want a fuck buddy. I wanted Claire. I sighed.

"What are you thinking about?" asked Janie in a seductive voice.

I stubbed out my cigarette and lit another immediately. "Oh, nothing." I could tell from her body language she knew what thoughts I was entertaining. Her mouth twitched angrily. "What about you? What are you thinking about while lying naked under the covers?" I tried coaxing her with a smile and eagerly taking in her slender leg with my eyes.

"You have it bad, don't you?" Janie sat up against the headboard and pulled the blanket to cover her entire body.

"What do you mean?" I had a feeling what she meant but felt no desire to talk about Claire.

Janie started to laugh maliciously. "You know, for someone who's supposed to be brilliant, you really are dumb. I can't believe I fucked the Miracle Girl and she has no clue who I am."

This piqued my curiosity somewhat. Something told me that the next few minutes of my life were going to be intense. My brain sent warning vibrations to every part of my body, but I sat there listless not giving a damn. The only thing I managed to accomplish was to fiddle with my phone, making her think I was stalling for time and not letting on that I was recording the conversation.

"Yeah?" I croaked. "Tell me, who are you, Janie?" It was hard to dig deep to summon the energy to probe and to speak loud enough for the mic.

"Ever hear of Senator Fuchs?" The look in her eyes annoyed the shit out of me. She eyed me like I was a cornered rat about to die. This helped me muster some energy to pay closer attention.

"Of course. You related or something?" I tapped my cigarette out the window and watched the ash float away on the wind.

Senator Fuchs from New Hampshire wanted to be the next President of the United States. His aspirations were grand considering the only thing he had going for him was he was running his campaign in New Hampshire, a key state when it came to early primaries. Most despised the Republican who wasn't even from the Granite State. He'd moved there for political ambitions and now wanted the assistance of everyone who lived there.

"No. Not related. I work for him."

"That's interesting." I flicked more ash out the window, wishing I could float away that easily. "Why are you in Colorado, then?"

"For you, of course."

I cocked my head and inhaled deeply on my Marlboro Light. "Senator Fuchs thinks I'm important. That's flattering." My brain was working overtime now to figure out how I'd been fooled.

"I'm amazed how easy it was to bed you, really. I think the senator should write Claire a thank you note."

It took every ounce of control not to flinch. I kept every muscle in my body relaxed, not wanting to let on she was getting under my skin. If I showed weakness now, I was toast. Sayo-fucking-nara.

"Maybe I should thank the Senator as well. You're an incredible fuck."

Janie looked pleased with the compliment.

"You too, my dear. If you didn't have Claire on the brain, I may have reported back that I failed. I think you're the type of person I could fall for, really." Her eyes told me she wasn't flattering me to soften me up. Janie had the look of a young woman who was absolutely convinced she could sway me to get over Claire. Only the young could manage that level of confidence.

"Another time, another place. Isn't that usually the case?" I flicked my cigarette out the window. "So what exactly is your mission?" I lit another cigarette.

"Tad wants Beale Media Corp to back his campaign."

I burst into laughter. "You've got to be joking. They'll never back such a prick and a Republican!"

"That's where you come in, Miracle Girl."

I shook my head, not understanding. "I run a dying paper in the West. I'm not exactly running the show at headquarters."

"No, but you're Cora's Miracle Girl. And after all those AA meetings when you sobbed to everyone about Claire and how you got the moniker, well, let's just say I knew I hit a fucking grand slam." She mimicked swinging a bat. "Besides, everyone knows they're grooming you to take over for Cora." The menacing gleam was back in her eyes. Fucking hostess at a steak joint. I'd fallen for that.

"You're not an addict, are you?"

She shook her head.

"And I guess you won't honor the code. Not speaking about what's said in meetings."

"That depends on you."

"Ah, I see. If Senator Fuchs doesn't get his endorsement, you'll out how and why I got the name and Cora's role." I nodded, appreciatively. Oh, the irony was too much. Cora had forced me back into AA, instructing me to bare my soul to fellow addicts, and now this. I wanted to laugh.

"Now you're getting it. Maybe you aren't just a good fuck after all. I even have photos of the tattoo on your back. It'll go well with the story, I think. Tortured executive kicks cocaine while reeling from … That's right, you don't know what happened to you that one night. Raped? Prostituted yourself? Or just an out of control drug-induced orgy? You have no fucking clue. The tabloids will love it. And of course, we'll produce 'witnesses.'"

Flicking the half-smoked cigarette out the window, I moved to sit on the bed next to her, slipping my finger under the sheet and tracing it up her naked body. "It's a shame really." I had to play this right. The clock was ticking.

"What is?"

"I liked sleeping with you."

Janie whipped the covers off exposing herself once again and flashing that look that claimed she could take all my pain away if I just gave her a chance. Be with her. Leaning down I took her nipple in my mouth, biting it. She gasped, relieved.

"So we have an understanding, then?" she asked.

"Oh, yes. I understand everything. It's been a long time since I've seen things this clearly."

I fucked her for the last time.

Seconds after Janie left my place I rolled over in bed and grabbed my cell phone.

Cora's raspy voice snapped, "This better be important."

"Stop the presses."

I could almost see her bolt upright in bed. "What have you done, JJ?"

"Found a way to end the charade."

"What charade?"

"The Miracle Girl scam, of course. It's time I shed my past completely."

"What in the fuck are you talking about?"

"Boy have I got a story for you." I could already see the headlines.

"And I'm assuming this is also your way of committing career suicide."

"Most definitely."

"Why should I agree to it then? We're talking about my career as well."

"Because it's a great story. Sex, drugs, corruption, presidential hopeful, and we have the scoop. My paper has the scoop."

She sighed. "It's no secret I'm on my way out. What do you need from me?"

"Get the people I need in the office. Our best writer, George. Avery.

Brenda—"

"Brenda?"

"Trust me on this. She looks like a kook, but she knows her stuff. She should be my replacement, along with Avery." I could picture Cora jotting everything down. "I'll be in the office in an hour. I have to stop by my parents' first. Prepare them for the media storm."

She was silent for a moment. "Jesus, you're really going to do this, aren't you?"

chapter twenty-one

I sat in the restaurant, wondering why Darrell wanted to meet with me. I had hoped I would never have to see him again. Less than a week after the exposé, he called and insisted on meeting. For some insane reason I agreed. Maybe it was the newspaper woman in me. Not that I had a job anymore. It was decided it was best for the company if I resigned immediately. I agreed wholeheartedly. Cora and I planned on starting an online media company in the new year, but no word of that had leaked yet.

He slipped into the seat opposite me and nodded hello. The waiter immediately approached. "I'll have a Coors Light," said Darrel, and then he looked at me guiltily and corrected his order. "Actually, I have to drive later. I'll have a Coke."

I wanted to disappear into my seat, embarrassed that Darrell of all people felt like he couldn't order a beer because of me. I hated pity, and pity from him was too much.

The waiter retreated. "You can have a beer, you know."

Darrell started to speak, but changed his mind. He shifted in his seat, and I noticed he had a hard time getting comfortable. I remembered Claire saying he had football injuries and wondered how often he was in pain. I was sure the car wreck months ago didn't help matters.

"I have to give it to you, JJ. I thought I did a splendid job wrecking my career, but you went above and beyond." His thin lips curled up into a smile. "You okay?"

Darrell's concern floored me. Was that why he wanted to meet? To commiserate losing our standing in the publishing world? "Fine, thanks. It was a long time coming … for me, that is."

"And for me." He cleared his throat. "You were right. I couldn't see the writing on the wall. The newspaper business isn't what it was twenty years ago. Hell, it's nothing like it was five years ago."

I smiled. The business changed almost daily with social media. "How is the newspaper business in Wyoming treating you?"

"Not bad. Not exciting, but I'm learning not to expect much. The publisher has his own agenda, and I have a family to support."

The hint about Claire and Ian was like having hot lava poured over me after having all of my skin peeled away. I jolted in my seat, not that he noticed.

"That's why I came today."

"What is?" I asked.

"Claire."

I stared at him, unable to speak.

He put a hand up to silence me, even though I hadn't spoken a word nor had I made a move to speak. "Just hear me out for once, will ya?" Darrell's cocky smile irritated and intrigued me. "When Claire saw the news—about you and, well, there's no need to discuss the rest—she confessed to me why she left the paper."

I felt the room spin violently like I was drunk and was about to spew my guts all over the floor.

Darrell either didn't notice my distress or chose to ignore it completely. "She loves you. You do know that, don't you?" His eyes softened, and his tone implied he was trying to get me to see the error of my ways. "You should go to her. She's afraid to come to you."

"Why?" I croaked, barely able to get the word out. "You did a pretty decent job of sabotage. She thinks I threatened you at the hospital."

He paled and looked away. "No she doesn't. I told her what really happened. How I blackmailed you and how you called my bluff. By the way, that was masterful the way you handled that."

"When did you tell her?"

"The day the news broke about—" He pointed at me.

That was four days ago. "Why hasn't she called?"

He shrugged. "Probably the same reason you've haven't. Fear of rejection. Isn't that what we all fear?"

Neither of us spoke.

He broke the spell. "Did it work?"

"What?"

"Did you save the paper?"

I laughed. "Kinda. Cora extended the deadline another six months before making the decision. She wants to see how everything plays out."

He nodded.

I knew Cora was leaving at the end of the year and didn't want to be the one to close the paper I gave up everything for. Word was Beale Media Corp was looking for a buyer for *Mile High*, and with all the hoopla I'd generated, hopes were high someone would bite.

I LOOKED AT the address scrawled in Darrell's writing. It had taken me two days to get up the nerve to see Claire. I decided against giving her any advance warning, but Darrell assured me she didn't leave the office until seven each night when Ian was with him.

It was just after seven, and I leaned against her car in the *Fort Collins Gazette* parking lot.

As I saw her exit the building, I realized my legs were shaking.

Claire was on the phone, but when she saw me, she stopped everything, including speaking. Then I heard her say, "Can I call you back tomorrow?" She ended the call.

She didn't speak.

Neither did I.

This wasn't going as I'd hoped.

"Hello," she said in a tone that puzzled me. Was it frosty? Or nervous?

"Hi, Claire," I said like an awkward teenager.

"JJ." She nodded her head.

This really wasn't going well.

"Would you like to come in?" She pointed to the office building.

"I was hoping I could take you to dinner." I wanted to be on neutral turf.

She looked conflicted. After a few seconds, she nodded and approached me slowly.

Nervously, I pointed to my car.

She shook her head, making me smile.

I grabbed her arm and pulled her toward me. Claire didn't fight me, and I wrapped her in my arms. "God I missed you." I rested my head against her chest.

"Why didn't you come sooner?" she whispered.

"I had to sever all ties to my past first," I babbled between sobs. "I didn't know it at the time, but now I do."

"Even me."

I looked up at her. "So I could be with you."

"And you think you can waltz back into my life, just like that." She backed away from me.

"No. Not just like that. I'll do whatever you say, and I'll wait however long you need."

She didn't move a muscle. Both of us stood, staring at each other.

"Just give me a chance to prove myself."

Still, she gave me zero indication of what she was thinking.

"It took guts to go public about the reasons behind the label," she said.

"I should have done it years ago. It wasn't until I confessed publically that I realized how much it was holding me back. Look, I can turn my head completely to the left. I haven't been able to do that in years. No more Bengay."

She nodded. A slight smile was creeping onto her face.

"And now I want to focus on the future. Not the past."

Claire crossed her arms.

"What are your plans?"

I laughed. "I'm looking for a house in Colorado. Know any good neighborhoods up here?"

She jutted her chin out. "You're not moving back to New York?"

I shook my head. "I'm not running this time."

Claire blinked. And then blinked some more. "You're in luck. They recently opened an Olive Garden just down the street." With that, she walked to the passenger side of my car and waited for me to unlock the door.

I climbed into the driver's seat of my SUV.

Claire had opened the door for me, and I wasn't going to blow my third chance.

I turned the key in the ignition. "How have you been?"

"Better now. Much better."

I rested my hand on her thigh.

Claire laughed. "I do plan on making you work for it."

Leaning back in the car seat I said, "I'm committed, one hundred percent."

"That's good to know, Jamilla Jean."

"You know, that name doesn't sound that bad coming from you."

Claire placed her hand on mine. "Darrell told me the truth. I had no idea you were protecting me and Ian. I should have trusted you."

I squeezed her hand. "And I should have told you everything. And I never should have had a drink. I know better. I just didn't know what to do that night."

She nodded her head. "So, what's the next step, Miss One Hundred Percent Committed?"

"Tonight, dinner to talk about us. Tomorrow, well I'm not sure yet. One day at a time, Claire. One day at a time."

"Saying it that way makes it less scary."

It did. I finally realized that.

"Being here, with you, makes everything worth it."

"Can you pull the car over, please?" The urgency in her voice rattled me.

"Sure. Is everything okay?" I pulled into a deserted church parking lot.

Claire didn't respond. Instead, she pulled my head to hers and kissed me. It was a kiss that said she never wanted us to be apart again. She pulled away. "I don't want to go to Olive Garden. You remember the way to my parents' cabin?"

I nodded. "I could never forget anything associated with you."

"Use your New York driving skills and put the pedal to the medal. I need you. And I want to show you how much. We've wasted enough time."

Author's Note

Thank you for reading *The Miracle Girl.* If you enjoyed the novel, please consider leaving a review on Goodreads or Amazon. No matter how long or short, I would very much appreciate your feedback.

You can follow me, T. B. Markinson, on twitter at @50YearProject or email me at tbmarkinson@gmail.com. I would love to know your thoughts.

Acknowledgments

I would like to thank my editor, Jeri Walker-Bickett. I am extremely grateful for all the hours she spent hunting for my mistakes, and for her patience, insight, and guidance. Editors play a vital role in the publishing business, and many don't understand how wonderful it is to find an editor that is easy to work with and who understands the ins and outs of publishing. Erin Dameron-Hill designed a stunning cover. Lastly, my sincerest thanks go to all my blogging buddies who have cheered me on for the past four years. When I first heard of blogging I scoffed, thinking I would never take to it. It wasn't until I met so many wonderful people online who have been there for me through the best and worst times that I realized how wrong I was. I'm honored to call all of you my friends, and I'm so thankful I changed my tune about starting a blog.

About the Author

TB Markinson is an American writer living in England. When she isn't writing, she's traveling the world, watching sports on the telly, visiting pubs, or taking the dog for a walk—not necessarily in that order.

Manufactured by Amazon.ca
Bolton, ON